if she knew

(a kate wise mystery—book 1)

blake pierce

ISBN: 978-1-64029-793-7

BOOKS BY BLAKE PIERCE

KATE WISE MYSTERY SERIES
IF SHE KNEW (Book #1)

THE MAKING OF RILEY PAIGE SERIES
WATCHING (Book #1)
WAITING (Book #2)

RILEY PAIGE MYSTERY SERIES
ONCE GONE (Book #1)
ONCE TAKEN (Book #2)
ONCE CRAVED (Book #3)
ONCE LURED (Book #4)
ONCE HUNTED (Book #5)
ONCE PINED (Book #6)
ONCE FORSAKEN (Book #7)
ONCE COLD (Book #8)
ONCE STALKED (Book #9)
ONCE LOST (Book #10)
ONCE BURIED (Book #11)
ONCE BOUND (Book #12)
ONCE TRAPPED (Book #13)
ONCE DORMANT (Book #14)

MACKENZIE WHITE MYSTERY SERIES
BEFORE HE KILLS (Book #1)
BEFORE HE SEES (Book #2)
BEFORE HE COVETS (Book #3)
BEFORE HE TAKES (Book #4)
BEFORE HE NEEDS (Book #5)
BEFORE HE FEELS (Book #6)
BEFORE HE SINS (Book #7)
BEFORE HE HUNTS (Book #8)
BEFORE HE PREYS (Book #9)

AVERY BLACK MYSTERY SERIES
CAUSE TO KILL (Book #1)
CAUSE TO RUN (Book #2)
CAUSE TO HIDE (Book #3)

CAUSE TO FEAR (Book #4)
CAUSE TO SAVE (Book #5)
CAUSE TO DREAD (Book #6)

KERI LOCKE MYSTERY SERIES
A TRACE OF DEATH (Book #1)
A TRACE OF MUDER (Book #2)
A TRACE OF VICE (Book #3)
A TRACE OF CRIME (Book #4)
A TRACE OF HOPE (Book #5)

PROLOGUE

He saw no one watching him as he crept down the quiet suburban street at night. It was one in the morning and it was the kind of neighborhood where people went to bed at respectable times, a rowdy weeknight consisting of one too many glasses of wine while watching *The Bachelor*.

It was the kind of place he despised.

They paid property association dues, they scooped up their dogs' shit into little plastic bags as to not offend their neighbors, and their kids surely played sports not just in high school leagues but in private county leagues. The world was their oyster. They felt safe. Sure, they locked their doors and set their alarms, but ultimately, they felt safe.

That was about to change.

He walked up a particular lawn. Surely she would be home now. Her husband was away on business in Dallas. He knew which window was her bedroom window. And he also knew that the security alarm at the back of the house was faulty when it rained.

He shifted and felt the reassurance of the knife, tucked away in the small of his back, between the elastic of his boxer shorts and his jeans. He stuck to the side of the house, opening the bottle of water he carried, and when he came to the back of the house, he stopped. There was the glowing green light of the small security box. He knew that if he tried to damage it, the alarm would go off. He knew if he tried to open a door or pry it open, the alarm would go off.

But he also knew it messed up in the rain. It was something about the moisture, even though this type of system was supposed to be one hundred percent waterproof. With this in mind, he raised his bottle of water and doused it.

He watched as the little green light flickered, grew weak.

With a smile, he walked into the small strip of backyard. He made his way up the stairs of the screened in back porch. Using the knife to pry the screen door open was easy; it made very little noise in the quiet of the night.

He crossed to the wicker chair in the corner, lifted the cushion, and found the key underneath. He picked it up in his gloved hand, went to the back door, slid the key in, turned the lock, and stepped inside.

A small lamp was on in the thin hallway that ran out of the kitchen. He followed this hall to a stairway, and he began to climb.

Anxiety swirled in his guts. He was getting excited—not in a sexual way but in the way he used to get excited when he rode a roller coaster, the anticipation thrilling him as he ascended, clacking up the biggest hill on the tracks.

He gripped the knife, still in his hand from having pried open the screen door. At the top of the stairs he took a moment to appreciate the thrill of it. He breathed in the cleanliness of the upper-class suburban home and it made him a little sick. It was too familiar, too detached.

He hated it.

Gripping the knife, he walked to the bedroom at the end of the hall. There she was, lying in the bed.

She was sleeping on her side, her knees slightly bent. She was wearing a T-shirt and a pair of running shorts, nothing too impressive being that her husband was gone.

He walked to the bed and watched her sleep for a while. He wondered about the nature of life. How fragile it was.

He then raised the knife and brought it down almost casually, as if he were simply painting or swatting a fly.

She screamed, but only for a moment—before he brought the knife down again.

And again.

CHAPTER ONE

Of the many life lessons her first full year of retirement had taught Kate Wise, the most important was this: without a solid plan, retirement could get boring very fast.

She'd heard stories of women who had retired and picked up different interests. Some opened up little Etsy shops online. Some dabbled in painting and crochet. Others tried their hand at writing a novel. Kate thought these were all fine ways to pass the time, but none of them appealed to her.

For someone who had spent more than thirty years of her life with a gun strapped to her side, finding ways to be happily preoccupied was difficult. Knitting was not going to replace the thrill of an on-foot pursuit of a killer. Gardening was not going to recreate the adrenaline high of storming into a residence, never knowing what waited on the other side of the door.

Because nothing she tried seemed to even come close to touching the joy she had felt as an FBI agent, she had stopped searching after a couple of months. The only thing that even came close were her trips to the gun range, which she made twice a week. She would have made more if she didn't fear that the younger members at the range might start to think of her as nothing more than a retired agent who was trying to recapture a moment in time when she had been great.

It was a reasonable fear. After all, she supposed that's exactly what she was doing.

It was a Tuesday, just after two in the afternoon, when this fact struck her like a bullet between the eyes. She had just come back from the range and was setting her M1911 pistol back in her bedside drawer when her heart seemed to break out of nowhere.

Thirty-one years. She'd spent thirty-one years with the bureau. She'd been a part of more than one hundred raids and had worked as part of a special enforcement unit for high-profile cases on twenty-six occasions. She'd been known for her speed, her quick and often razor-sharp thinking, and her overall don't-give-a-damn attitude.

She'd also been known for her looks, something that still bothered her a bit even at the age of fifty-five. When she'd become an agent at the age of twenty-three, it had not taken her long to get crude nicknames like Legs and Barbie—names that would likely get men fired these days but which, back when she had been younger, had sadly been commonplace for female agents.

Kate had broken noses at the bureau because male agents would grab her ass. She had thrown one across a moving elevator when he'd whispered something obscene in her ear while behind her.

While the nicknames had stayed with her until well into her forties, the advances and leering looks had not. After word had gotten around, her male peers had learned to respect her and to look beyond her body—a body which, she knew with some degree of muted pride, had always been well-maintained and what most men would consider a ten.

But now at fifty-five she found herself missing even the nicknames. She had not thought retirement would be this hard. The gun range was fine, but it was just a whispering ghost of what her past had been. She had tried to shove the yearning for her past away by reading. She had decided she would read up on weapons in particular; she'd read countless books about the history of weapons use, how they were manufactured, the preference for certain weapons by military generals, and the like. It was why she now used an M1911, because of its rich history with being involved in a multitude of American wars, an early model of it being used as far back as World War I.

She'd tried her hand at reading fiction but could not get into it—though she did enjoy a lot of the cybercrime–related books. While she *had* revisited books she'd adored in her younger years, she could find nothing interesting in the lives of fake characters. And because she had not wanted to become the sad recently retired lady who spent all of her time at the local library, she'd ordered all of the books she'd read in the last year off of Amazon. She had more than one hundred of them stacked in boxes in her basement. She figured one day she'd build a few bookcases and turn the space into a proper study.

It wasn't like she had much else to do.

Rocked by the idea that she had spent the last year of her life doing not much of anything, Kate Wise sat slowly down on her bed. She stayed there for several minutes without moving. She looked to the desk across the room and saw the photo albums there. There was only a single family picture there. In it, her late husband, Michael, had his arms around their daughter while Kate smiled at his side. A picture from the beach that was poorly taken but had always warmed her heart.

4

All of the other pictures in those albums, however, were from work: behind-the-scenes shots, pictures of inner-bureau birthday parties, her in her younger years swimming laps, at the gun range, running track, and so on.

She had lived the last year of her life the same way the small-town jock who never leaves his small town would. Always hanging around anyone who would pretend to listen about all of the touchdowns he'd scored thirty years ago playing high school football.

She was no better than that.

With a slight shudder, Kate got up and went to the photo albums on her desk. Slowly and almost methodically, she looked through all three of them. She saw pictures of her younger self, evolving through the years until every picture ever taken was on a phone. She saw herself and people she had known, people who had died right beside her on cases, and started to realize that while these moments had been instrumental in developing her, they had not defined her completely.

The articles she had clipped and saved in the back of the album further told the story. She was the featured story in all of them. SECOND-YEAR AGENT NABS KILLER ON THE LOOSE read one title; FEMALE AGENT LONE SURVIVOR IN SHOOTOUT THAT CLAIMED 11. And then the one that had really started spurring the legends on: AFTER 13 VICTIMS, MOONLIGHT KILLER FINALLY TAKEN DOWN BY AGENT KATE WISE.

By all reasonable health standards, she had at least twenty more years in her—forty if she could somehow manage to really buckle down and fight death away. Even if she averaged it out and said she had *thirty* years left, kicking the bucket at eighty-five…thirty years was a lot.

She could do a lot in thirty years, she supposed. For about ten of those years, she could maybe even have some very good years before old age really started to sneak in and start plucking away her good health.

The question, of course, was what she might find to do with those years.

And despite having a reputation as one of the sharpest agents to go through the bureau in the last decade, she had no idea where to start.

***

5

Aside from the gun range and her almost obsessive reading habits, Kate had also managed to make a weekly habit out of meeting with three other women for coffee. The four of them made fun of themselves, claiming they had formed the saddest club ever: four women early in retirement with no idea what to do with their newly freed up days.

The day following her revelation, Kate drove to their coffee house of choice. It was a little family-owned place where not only was the coffee better than the overpriced gruel at Starbucks, but the place wasn't overrun with millennials and soccer moms. She walked inside and before she went to the counter to place her order, she saw their usual table in the back. Two of the three other women were already there, waving to her.

Kate grabbed her hazelnut brew and joined her friends at the table. She sat down beside Jane Patterson, a fifty-seven-year-old who was seven months retired from springing back and forth between companies as a proposal specialist for a government telecommunications firm. Across from her was Clarissa James, a little over a year into retirement ever since working part-time as a criminology instructor with the bureau. The fourth member of their sad little club, a fifty-five-year-old recently retired woman named Debbie Meade, had not yet shown up.

Odd, Kate thought. *Deb is usually the first one here.*

The moment she took her seat, Jane and Clarissa seemed to go tense. This was particularly weird because it was not like Clarissa to be anything other than bubbly. Unlike Kate, Clarissa had quickly grown to love retirement. Kate supposed it helped that Clarissa was married to a man nearly ten years younger than her who competed in swimming competitions in his free time.

"What's with you guys?" Kate asked. "You know I come here to try to get motivated about retirement, right? You two look downright sad."

Jane and Clarissa shared a look that Kate had seen countless times before. During her times as an agent, she'd seen it in living rooms, interrogation rooms, and hospital waiting rooms. It was a look that translated one simple question without a spoken word: *Who's going to tell her?*

"What is it?" she asked.

She was suddenly very aware of Deb's absence.

"It's Deb," Jane said, confirming her fear.

"Well, not Deb exactly," Clarissa added. "It's her daughter, Julie. Did you ever meet her?"

"Once, I think," Kate said. "What happened?"

6

"She's dead," Clarissa said. "Murder. So far, they have no idea who did it."

"Oh my God," Kate said, genuinely saddened for her friend. She'd known Deb for about fifteen years, having met her at Quantico. Kate had been working as an assistant instructor for a new crop of field agents and Deb had been working with some of the tech rats on some sort of new security system. They'd struck it off right away and had become fast friends.

The fact that Deb had not called or texted her with the news before anyone else showed just how quickly friendships could shift over the years.

"When did it happen?" Kate asked.

"Sometime yesterday," Jane said. "She just texted me this morning about it."

"They have *no* suspects?" Kate asked.

Jane shrugged. "She just said they don't know who it is. No clues, no leads, nothing."

Kate instantly felt herself go into agent mode. She figured it was the same way a trained athlete must feel after being away from their arena of choice for too long. She may not have turf or an adoring crowd to remind her of what her glory days had been like, but she *did* have her finely tuned mind for solving crimes.

"Don't go there," Clarissa said, trying on her best smile.

"Go where?"

"Don't be Agent Wise right now," Clarissa said. "Right now, just be her friend. I can see those wheels turning in your head. Jeez, lady. Don't you have a pregnant daughter? Aren't you about to be a grandmother?"

"What a way to kick me when I'm down," Kate said with a smile. She let the comment go and then asked: "Deb's daughter...did she have a boyfriend?"

"No idea," Jane said.

An awkward silence sat over the table. In the year or so their little group of recently retired friends had been meeting, the conversation had always been mostly light. This was the first heavy topic and it did not fit with their routine. Kate, of course, was accustomed to it. Her time in the academy had taught her how to handle these situations.

But Clarissa was right. In hearing the news, Kate had so easily slipped into agent mode. She knew she should have thought like a friend first—thinking of Deb's loss and emotional state. But the agent in her was too strong, the instincts still there at the forefront after having been on the shelf for a year.

"So what can we do to make her comfortable?" Jane asked.

"I was thinking a meal train," Clarissa said. "I know a few other ladies that might get on board. Just making sure she doesn't have to cook for her family in the next few weeks as she deals with all of this."

For the next ten minutes, the three women planned out the most effective way to get a meal train going for their grief-stricken friend.

But for Kate, the conversation remained on the surface. Her mind was headed elsewhere, trying to dig up hidden facts and tidbits on Deb and her family, trying to find a case where there might not even be one.

Or there might, Kate thought. *And I guess there's only one way to find out.*

CHAPTER TWO

After retirement, Kate had moved back to Richmond, Virginia. She'd grown up in the little town of Amelia, about forty minutes away from Richmond, but had gone to college right near the cusp of downtown. She'd spent her undergrad years at VCU, originally wanting to be an art major of all things. Three years in, she'd discovered that she'd had a heart for criminal justice through one of her elective courses in psychology. It had been a winding, crooked trail that had led her to Quantico and the thirty-year stretch of her illustrious career.

She now drove through some of those familiar Richmond streets. She'd been to Debbie Meade's house only once before but knew exactly where it was located. She knew where it was because she envied the location, one of those older-looking buildings on the streets off the center of downtown that were lined with trees rather than street lights and tall buildings.

Deb's street was currently awash in fallen leaves from the elms that overhung the street. She had to park three houses away because family and friends had already started to fill in the spaces in front of Deb's house.

She walked down the sidewalk, trying to convince herself that this was a bad idea. Yes, she planned to enter the house as only a friend—even though Jane and Clarissa had decided to hold off until later in the afternoon in order to give Deb some space. But there was something deeper there, too. She'd been looking for something to do these past few months, some better and more meaningful way to fill her time. She'd often dreamed about somehow picking up freelance work from the bureau, maybe even just basic research tasks.

Even the most minor of references to her work got her excited. For instance, she was due in court next week to testify at a parole hearing. She was not looking forward to facing the criminal again but just being able to delve back into her work for such a brief amount of time was welcome.

But that was next week—and right now that seemed like an eternity away.

She looked up at Debbie Meade's front porch. She knew why she was really there. She wanted to find some answers to questions

9

that were storming in her head. It made her feel selfish, like she was using her friend's loss as an excuse to dip her toes back into waters that she had not felt in over a year. This situation involved a friend, which made it tricky. But the old agent in her was hoping it might evolve into something else. The friend in her, though, thought it might be risky. And all together, those parts of her wondered if maybe she should have stuck with simply fanaticizing about a return to work.

Maybe that's exactly what I'm doing, Kate thought as she walked up the stairs to the Meade residence. And honestly, she wasn't quite sure how to feel about that.

She knocked on the door softly and it was answered right away by an elderly lady Kate did not know.

"Are you with the family?" the woman asked.

"No," Kate answered. "Just a very close friend."

The woman scrutinized her for a moment before allowing her inside. Kate entered and walked down the hallway, passing by a living area that was filled with somber people sitting around one single person in a recliner. The person in the recliner was Debbie Meade. Kate recognized the man standing beside her and talking to another man as her husband, Jim.

She awkwardly entered the room and went directly to Deb. Without allowing Deb enough time to get out of the chair, Kate leaned down and hugged her.

"I'm so sorry, Deb," she said.

Deb was clearly drained from crying, managing to only nod into Kate's shoulder. "Thanks for coming," Deb whispered into her ear. "Do you think you could meet me in the kitchen in a few minutes?"

"Of course."

Kate broke the hug and gave little nods of acknowledgment to the few other faces in the room that she recognized. Feeling out of place, Kate made her way to the end of the hallway which emptied into the kitchen. There was no one there but there were empty plates and glasses from where people had been not too long ago. There were a few pies sitting on the counter along with ham rolls and other finger foods. Kate set to cleaning up, helping herself to the sink to start washing the dishes.

Several moments later, Jim Meade made his way into the kitchen. "You don't have to do that," he said.

Kate turned to him and saw that he looked tired and impossibly sad. "I know," she said. "I came by to show my support. It seemed like things were pretty heavy in the living room when I came in, so I'm supporting you guys by washing dishes."

He nodded, looking like he might nod off right then and there. "One of our friends said she saw a woman come in a few minutes ago. I'm rather glad it's you, Kate."

Kate saw another person coming toward the kitchen behind him, looking equally tired and heartbroken. Deb Meade's eyes were puffy and red from crying. Her hair was in disarray and when she looked at Kate to try on a smile, it seemed to fall right off of her face.

Kate put down the dish she was washing, quickly dried her hands on a hand towel by the sink, and went to her friend. Kate had never been much for physical touch but knew when a hug was needed. She expected Deb to start weeping in the midst of the hug but there was nothing, just her sagging weight.

She's probably all cried out for now, Kate thought.

"I only just heard this morning," Kate said. "I'm so sorry, Deb. Both of you," she said, casting her eyes to Jim.

Jim nodded his appreciation and then looked down the hall. When he saw that no one else was lurking there, the slight murmur of their company still in the living room, he stepped closer to Kate as Deb broke the hug.

"Kate, we need to ask you something," Jim said in a near-whisper.

"And please," Deb said, taking her hand. "Let us get it all out before you shoot us down." Kate felt a little tremble in Deb's grip and her heart broke a little.

"Sure," Kate said. Their pleading eyes and the overall weight of their sorrow hung over her head like an anvil that was sure to drop at any moment.

"The police have absolutely no idea who did it," Deb said. Suddenly, her exhaustion morphed into something that looked closer to anger. "Based on some things we said and some texts they found on Julie's phone, the police arrested her ex-boyfriend right away. But they held him for less than three hours and then let him go. Just like that. But Kate...I *know* he did it. It *has* to be him."

Kate had seen this approach multiple times before during her time as an agent. Grieving families wanted justice right away. They'd look past logic and a sound investigation to make sure some sort of vengeance was taken out as soon as possible. And if those results weren't speedy, the grieving family assumed incompetence on the part of the police or FBI.

"Deb…if they released him so quickly, there must have been some very strong evidence. After all…how long has it been since they dated?"

"Thirteen years. But he kept trying to connect with her for years, even after she was married. She had to get a restraining order at one time."

"Still…the police had to have a good alibi for him to have released him so quickly."

"Well, if there was, they aren't telling me about it," Deb said.

"Deb…look," Kate said, giving Deb's hand a comforting squeeze. "The loss is too recent. Give it a few days and you'll start to think rationally. I've seen it a hundred times."

Deb shook her head. "I'm certain of it, Kate. They dated for three years and not once did I trust him. We're pretty sure he hit her at least on two occasions but Julie never came out and said it. He had a temper. Even *he'd* tell you that."

"I'm sure the police are—"

"That's our favor," Deb interrupted. "I want *you* to look into it. I want you to get involved in the case."

"Deb, I'm retired. You know this."

"I do. And I also know how much you miss it. Kate…the man that killed my daughter got nothing more than a little scare and some time in an interrogation room. And now he's at home, sitting comfortably while I have to plan to put my daughter in the ground. It's not right, Kate. Please…will you look into it? I know you can't do it on an official basis but…anything you can do. I'd appreciate it."

There was so much heartache in Deb's eyes that Kate could feel it passing between them. Everything within her was telling her to stand firm—to not allow any false hope to enter into Deb's grief. But at the same time, Deb was right. She *had* missed her work. And even if what was being proposed was just a few basic phone calls to the Richmond PD or even to her former co-workers at the bureau, it would be *something.*

It would certainly be better than obsessively reflecting back on her career with lonely trips out to the gun range.

"Here's what I can do," Kate said. "When I retired, I lost all of my pull. Sure, I get calls for my opinion here and there, but I have no authority. More than that, this case would be completely outside of my jurisdiction even if I *were* still active. But I will make a few calls to my old contacts and make sure the evidence they found to free him was strong. Honestly, Deb, that's the best I can do."

The gratitude was evident in both Deb and Jim right away. Deb hugged her again and this time, she did weep. "Thank you."

"It's not a problem," Kate said. "But I really can't promise anything."

"We know," Jim said. "But at least now we know that someone competent is watching out for us."

Kate wasn't comfortable with the idea that they were looking to her as an inside force to assist them, nor did she like that they assumed the police didn't have their backs. Again, she knew it was all about their grief and how it was blinding them in their search for answers. So for now, she let it slide.

She thought about how tired she had been near the end of her career—not really physically tired but emotionally drained. She had always loved her job, but how often had she come to the end of a case and think to herself: *Man, am I tired of this shit...*

It had happened more and more often in the last few years.

But this moment was not about her.

She held her friend close, puzzling over how no matter how hard people tried to put their pasts behind them—whether it was relationships or careers—it somehow managed to always limp along not too far behind.

CHAPTER THREE

Kate wasted no time. She returned home and sat at the desk in her small study for a moment. She looked out of her study window, into her small backyard. Sunshine came in through the window, laying a rectangle of light on her wooden floors. The floors, like most of the rest of the house, showed the scars and scabs of its 1920s construction. Located in the Carytown area of Richmond, Kate often felt out of place. Carytown was a trendy little section of the city and she knew she'd end up moving elsewhere fairly soon. She had enough money to get a house just about anywhere she wanted but the very idea of moving exhausted her.

It was that sort of lack of motivation that had perhaps made retirement so hard for her. That and a refusal to let go of the memories of who she had been while with the bureau for those thirty years. When those two feelings collided, she often felt unmotivated and without any real direction.

But now there was Deb and Jim Meade's request. Yes, it was a misguided request but Kate saw nothing wrong with at least making a few calls. If it came to nothing, she could at least call Deb back to let her know that she had tried her best.

Her first call was to the Deputy Commissioner of the Virginia State Police, a man named Clarence Greene. She had worked closely with him on several cases over the last decade or so of her career and they shared a mutual respect for one another. She hoped the year that had passed had not totally obliterated that relationship. Knowing that Clarence was never in his office, she opted to skip his landline and called his cell phone.

Just when she thought the call was not going to be answered, she was greeted with a familiar voice. For a moment, Kate felt as if she had never left work at all.

"Agent Wise," Clarence said. "How the hell are you?"

"Good," she said. "You?"

"Same as always. I have to admit, though…I thought I was done with seeing your name pop up on my phone."

"Yeah, about that," Kate said. "I hate to come to you with something like this after more than a year of silence, but I have a friend who just lost her daughter. I gave her my word that I would look into the investigation."

"So what do you want from me?" Clarence asked.

"Well, the main suspect was the daughter's ex-boyfriend. It seems that he was arrested and then let go in about three hours. Naturally, the parents are wondering why."

"Oh," Clarence said. "Look…Wise, I can't really divulge that to you. And with all due respect, you should already know that."

"I'm not trying to interfere in the case," Kate said. "I was just wondering why no real reason has been given to the parents for letting the only suspect go. She's a grieving mom looking for answers and—"

"Again, let me stop you there," Clarence said. "As you well know, I deal with grieving moms and fathers and widows pretty regularly. Just because you happen to know one personally right now doesn't mean I can break protocol or look the other way."

"As closely as you've worked with me, you know I mean only the best."

"Oh, I'm sure you do. But the last thing I need is a retired FBI agent poking around in a current case, no matter how hands-off it may seem. You have to understand that, right?"

The hell of it was that she *did* understand it. Still, she had to try one last time. "I'd consider it a personal favor."

"I'm sure you would," Clarence said, a bit condescending. "But the answer is no, Agent Wise. Now if you'll excuse me, I'm about to head into court to speak to one of those grieving widows I just told you about. Sorry I couldn't help you."

He ended the call without a goodbye, leaving Kate to stare at that slowly shifting square of sunlight on the hardwood floor. She considered her next move, noting that Deputy Commissioner Greene had just revealed that he was about to head into court. She supposed the smart move would be to take his refusal to help her as a defeat. But his unwillingness to help only made her desire to keep digging that much stronger.

I was always told I had a stubborn streak as an agent, she thought as she stood up from her desk. *It's good to see that some things haven't changed.*

***

Half an hour later, Kate was parking her car in a parking garage adjacent to the Third Precinct Police Station. Based on where the murder of Julie Meade—married name Julie Hicks—had occurred, Kate knew it would be the best resource for information. The only problem was that aside from Deputy Commissioner Greene, she didn't really know anyone else within the department, much less the Third Precinct.

She entered the office with confidence. She knew there were certain things about her current situation that an observant officer would notice. First of all, she did not have her sidearm. She did have a concealed carry permit but given what she was up to, she figured it might cause more problems than it was worth if she was caught being even the slightest bit dishonest.

And dishonesty was really something she could not afford. Retired or not, her reputation was on the line—a reputation she had built with great care for over thirty years. She was going to have to walk a fine line in the next minutes, something she welcomed. She hadn't been this anxious in the entire year she had spent retired.

She approached the information desk, a brightly lit area separated from the central room by a pane of glass. A woman in uniform sat at the desk, stamping something in a ledger as Kate approached. She looked up at Kate with a face that looked as if a smile had not graced it in days.

"What can I do for you?" the receptionist asked.

"I'm a retired agent with the FBI, looking for some information about a recent murder. I was hoping to get the names of the officers in charge of the case."

"You got an ID?" the woman asked.

Kate got out her driver's license and slid it through the opening in the glass partition. The woman looked at it for a grand total of one second and then slid it right back. "I'm going to need your bureau ID."

"Well, like I said, I'm retired."

"And who sent you? I'll need their name and contact information and then they have to fill out a request to get you the information."

"I was really hoping to step over all of the legalities."

"I can't help you, then," the woman said.

Kate wondered how far she could push it. If she went too hard, someone would surely notify Clarence Greene and that could be bad. She racked her brain, trying to think of another course of action. She could only come up with one and it was much riskier than what she was currently attempting.

With a sigh, Kate gave a curt, "Well, thanks anyway."

She turned on her heel and walked back out of the office. She was a little embarrassed. What the hell had she been thinking? Even if she *did* still have her bureau ID, it would be unlawful for the

Richmond PD to give her any information without approval from a supervisor in DC.

It was beyond humbling to walk back out to her car with such an absolute feeling—the feeling of being a basic civilian.

But a civilian who hates to take no for an answer.

She took out her phone and placed a call to Deb Meade. When Deb answered, she still sounded tired and far away.

"Sorry to bother you, Deb," she said. "But do you have a name and address for the ex-boyfriend?"

As it turned out, Deb had both.

CHAPTER FOUR

While Kate did not have her old bureau ID, she did still have the last badge she had ever owned. It was propped up on the mantel over her fireplace like some relic from another time, no better than a faded photograph. When she left the Third Precinct station, she headed back home and scooped it up. She thought long and hard about also taking her sidearm. She looked longingly toward the M1911 but left it where it was in her bedside drawer. Taking it with her for what she had planned would be asking for trouble.

She did decide to take the handcuffs she kept in a shoebox under the bed with a few other treasures from her career.

Just in case.

She left her house and headed for the address Deb had given her. It was a place in Shockoe Bottom, a twenty-minute drive from her home. She was not nervous as she made the drive but she did feel a sense of excitement. She knew she should not be doing this, but at the same time, it felt good to be out and on the hunt again— even if it was in secret.

Just as she reached the address of Julie Hicks's former boyfriend, a guy named Brian Neilbolt, Kate thought about her husband. He popped up in her head from time to time but sometimes he seemed to pop up and sort of settle in for a while. That happened as she turned onto the destination street. He could see him shaking his head in frustration.

Kate, you know you shouldn't be doing this, he seemed to say.

She grinned thinly. She missed her husband fiercely sometimes, a fitting contrast to the fact that she sometimes felt she had managed to move on from his death rather quickly.

She shook the cobwebs of those memories away as she parked her car in front of the address Deb had given her. It was a rather nice house, split into two different apartments with porches separating the properties. When she got out of the car she could tell right away that someone was home because she could hear someone speaking very loudly inside.

When she climbed the porch stairs, she felt as if she had taken a step back in time, about one year ago. She felt like an agent again, despite the lack of the firearm on her hip. Still, being that she was in all actuality a retired agent, she had no idea what she would say after she knocked on the door.

But she didn't let that stop her. She knocked on the door with the same authority she would have one year ago. As she heard the loud talking inside, she figured she'd stick with the truth. Lying in a situation that she was already not supposed to be a part of would only make things worse if she was caught.

The man who answered the door took Kate a little off guard. He was about six feet three inches and was absolutely jacked. His shoulders alone showed that he worked out. He could have easily passed for a professional wrestler. The only thing that betrayed that façade was the anger in his eyes.

"Yeah?" he asked. "Who are you?"

She then made a move that she had missed very much. She showed him her badge. She hoped the sight of it would carry some weight to counter her introduction. "My name is Kate Wise. I'm a retired FBI agent. I was hoping you could speak with me for a few moments."

"About what?" he asked, his words quick and snappy.

"Are you Brian Neilbolt?" she asked.

"I am."

"So your ex-girlfriend was Julie Hicks, correct? Formerly Julie Meade?"

"Ah shit, this again? Look, the fucking cops already hauled me in and interrogated me. Now the feds, too?"

"Rest assured, I'm not here to interrogate you. I just wanted to ask some questions."

"Sounds like an interrogation to me," he said. "Besides, you said you're retired. Pretty sure that means I don't have to do anything you ask."

She pretended to be hurt by this, looking away from him. In reality, though, she was looking over his massive shoulders and the space behind him. She saw a suitcase and two backpacks leaning against the wall. She also saw a sheet of paper sitting on top of the suitcase. The large logo identified it as a printout of an Orbitz receipt. Apparently, Brian Neilbolt was leaving town for a while.

Not the best scenario for when your ex-girlfriend had been murdered and you had been taken in and then immediately released by the police.

"Where are you headed?" Kate asked.

"None of your business."

"Who were you talking to so loudly on the phone before I knocked?"

"Again, none of your business. Now, if you'll excuse me..."

He went to close the door, but Kate persisted. She stepped forward and wedged her shoe between the door and the frame. "Mr. Neilbolt, I'm only asking for about five minutes of your time."

A wave of fury passed through his eyes but then seemed to subside. He hung his head and for a moment, she thought he looked sad. It was similar to the look she had seen on the faces of the Meades.

"You said you're a retired agent, right?" Neilbolt asked.

"That's right," she confirmed.

"Retired," he said. "Then get the fuck off of my porch."

She stood resolute, making it clear that she had no intention of going anywhere.

"I said *get the fuck off of my porch!*"

He nodded and then reached out to push her. She felt the force of his hands when they struck her shoulder and acted as quickly as she could. Right away, she was amazed at how quickly her reflexes and muscle memory kicked in.

As she went stumbling backward, she wrapped both of her arms around Neilbolt's right arm. At the same time, she dropped to a knee to stop her backward momentum. She then did her best to hip toss him but his bulk was too much to handle. When he realized what she was trying to do, he threw a hard elbow into her ribs.

The breath went barreling out of Kate's chest but because he had thrown the elbow, his leverage was thrown off. This time when she attempted the hip toss, it worked. And because she put everything she had into it, it worked a little too well.

Neilbolt went sailing off the porch. When he landed, he hit the bottom two stairs. He cried out in pain and tried to get back to his feet right away. He looked up at her in shock, trying to figure out what had happened. Fueled by rage and surprise, he hobbled up the stairs toward her, clearly dazed.

She faked him out with a right knee to the face as he neared the top step. When he went to dodge it, she caught the side of his head and again went to her knees. She forced his head hard into the porch while his arms and legs scrambled for purchase on the stairs. She then freed the handcuffs from the interior of her jacket and applied them with a quickness and ease that only thirty years of experience can provide.

She stepped away from Brian Neilbolt and looked down at him. He was not fighting against the cuffs; he looked rather dazed, in fact.

Kate reached for her phone with the intention of calling the cops and realized that her hand was trembling. She was pumped up, flooded with adrenaline. She realized that there was a smile on her face.

God, I've missed this.

Although the blow to her ribs did hurt like hell—a lot more than it would have hurt five or six years ago for sure. And had the joints in her knees always ached this way after a skirmish?

She allowed herself a moment to revel in what she had done and then managed to finally make a call to the cops. Meanwhile, Brian Neilbolt remained groggy at her feet, perhaps wondering how a woman at least twenty years older than him had managed to so thoroughly hand his ass to him.

CHAPTER FIVE

Honestly, Kate had expected a little bit of blowback about what she had done, but nothing to the degree of what she experienced when she reached the Third Precinct Station. She knew something was coming when she saw the glances from the police who passed by in the midst of their office errands. Some of the looks were of awe while others stank of a sort of leering ridicule.

Kate let it slide right off of her back. She was still too riled up from the confrontation on Neilbolt's porch to care.

After she'd waited several minutes in the lobby, a nervous-looking officer approached her. "You're Ms. Wise, right?" he asked.

"I am."

A flash of recognition showed in his eyes. It was a look she had once gotten all the time when officers or agents who had only ever heard about her record met her for the first time. She missed that look.

"Chief Budd would like to speak to you."

She was frankly quite surprised. She was hoping to speak to someone more along the lines of Deputy Commissioner Greene. While he might have been a hard ass on the phone, she knew he could be persuaded more effectively in face-to-face meetings. Chief Randall Budd, though, was a no-nonsense kind of man. She'd only ever met him on one occasion a few years ago. She barely remembered the occurrence but *did* remember Budd leaving an impression of someone strong-willed and strictly professional.

Still, Kate did not want to seem intimidated or at all worried. So she got up and followed the officer out of the waiting area and back through the bullpen. They passed by several desks where she got more uncertain glances before the officer led her down a hallway. In the center of the hall they came to Randall Budd's office. The door was open, as if he had been waiting for her for quite some time.

The officer had nothing to say; once he had delivered her to Budd's doorway, he turned on his heel and left. Kate looked into the office and saw Chief Budd waving her in.

"Come on in," he said. "I won't lie. I'm not happy with you, but I don't bite. Close the door behind you, would you?"

Kate stepped inside and did as she was asked. She then took one of the three chairs that sat on the opposite side of Budd's desk. The desk was occupied with more personal effects than work-related items: pictures of his family, an autographed baseball, a personalized coffee mug, and some kind of sentimental shell casing sitting in a plaque.

"Let me start off by saying that I am well aware of your track record," Budd said. "More than one hundred arrests in your career. Top of your class in the academy. Gold and silver placement in eight consecutive kickboxing tournaments *in addition to* standard bureau training where you also kicked ass. Your name got around while you were running things and most of the people here in the Virginia State PD respect the hell out of you."

"But?" Kate said. She didn't say it in an attempt to be funny. She was simply letting him know that she was more than capable of being reprimanded...although she honestly didn't think she deserved much of it.

"But despite all that, you have no right to go around assaulting people just because you think they might have been involved in the death of one of your friend's daughters."

"I didn't visit him with intent to assault," Kate said. "I visited him to ask some questions. When he got physical with me, I simply defended myself."

"He told my men that you pitched him down the porch stairs and banged his head against the floor of the porch."

"I can't be blamed for being stronger than him, now can I?" she asked.

Budd looked closely at her, scrutinizing her. "I can't tell if you're trying to be funny, taking this lightly, or if this is really your everyday attitude."

"Chief, I understand your position and how a retired fifty-five-year-old woman beating up someone that your men had questioned briefly and then released could cause you a headache. But please understand...I only visited Brian Neilbolt because my friend asked me to. And honestly, when I learned a bit more about him, I thought it might not be a bad idea."

"So you just assumed my men didn't do an adequate job?" Budd asked.

"I said no such thing."

Budd rolled his eyes and sighed. "Look, I'm not trying to argue about it. Honestly, I would love nothing more than for you to leave my office in a few minutes and once we are done talking about this matter, it's done. I need you to understand, though, that you crossed

23

a line and if you happen to pull something like this again, I might just have to place you under arrest."

There were several things Kate wanted to say in response. But she figured if Budd was willing to press all arguments down, so could she. She knew that he was well within his power to really bring the hammer down on her if he wanted, so she decided to be as civil as possible.

"I understand," she replied.

Budd seemed to think about something for a moment before interlocking his hands together on the desk, as if trying to center himself. "And just so you know, we are certain that Brian Neilbolt did not kill Julie Hicks. We have him on security cameras outside of a bar on the night she was killed. He went in around ten and didn't leave until after midnight. We then have a text message trail between him and a current fling that went on between one and three in the morning. He checks out. He's not the guy."

"He had bags and suitcases packed," Kate pointed out. "Like he was trying to leave town in a hurry."

"In the text thread, he and this fling of his discussed visiting Atlantic City. They were supposed to be leaving this afternoon."

"I see." Kate nodded. She did not feel embarrassed per se, but she did start to regret acting so aggressively on Neilbolt's porch.

"There's one more thing," Budd said. "And again, you have to view things from my position on this. I had no choice but to contact your former supervisors at the FBI. It's protocol. Surely you know that."

She *did* know that but honestly had not thought about it. A slight yet gnawing irritation started to bloom in her guts.

"I know," she said.

"I spoke with Assistant Director Duran. He wasn't happy, and he wants to speak with you."

Kate rolled her eyes and nodded. "Fine. I'll give him a call and let him know it's from your instruction."

"No, you don't understand," Budd said. "They want to see you. In DC."

And with that, the irritation she was feeling quickly morphed into something she hadn't felt in a while: legitimate worry.

CHAPTER SIX

Following her meeting with Chief Budd, Kate made the appropriate calls to let her former supervisors know that she had received their request to visit them. She was not given any information over the phone and never actually spoke to anyone in power. That left her to leave a few rather rude messages with two unfortunate receptionists—an exercise that actually helped to relieve some of her stress.

She left Richmond the following morning at eight o'clock. She was curiously more excited than she was nervous. She figured it was kind of like a college graduate revisiting their campus after a brief time away. She'd missed the bureau terribly over the last year or so and was looking forward to being back in that environment...even if it was to be disciplined.

She distracted herself by listening to an obscure cinema-based podcast—a suggestion made by her daughter. Within five minutes of the podcast, the commentators had been drowned out and Kate was instead reflecting on the last few years of her life. For the most part, she was not a sentimental person but for some reason she had never understood, she tended to get nostalgic and reflective whenever she got on the road.

So instead of focusing on the podcast, she thought of her daughter—her pregnant daughter, due in about five weeks. The baby was to be a girl, named Michelle. The baby's father was a good enough man but, by Kate's estimation, had never quite been good enough for Melissa Wise. Melissa, called Lissa by Kate ever since she'd started to crawl, lived in Chesterfield, an area technically within Richmond but considered different by those who lived there. Kate had never told Melissa, but that was why she had moved back to Richmond. It had not been only because of her ties to the city due to her college experience, but because that was where her family was—where her first grandchild would live.

A grandchild, Kate often thought. *How did Melissa get that old? Hell, for that matter, how did I get that old?*

And when she thought of Melissa and the unborn Michelle, Kate typically turned her thoughts to her deceased husband. He'd been murdered six years ago, shot in the back of the head while walking their dog at night. His wallet and phone had been taken and she'd been called to ID the body less than two hours after he'd left the house with the dog.

The wound was still fresh most of the time but she hid it well. When she had retired from the bureau, she'd done so with about eight months left before official retirement age. But she had been unable to commit her full time, attention, and focus to her work after having finally scattered Michael's ashes over an old derelict baseball diamond near his home in Falls Church.

Perhaps that was why she had spent the last year so depressed about leaving her job. She had left months before she'd legally had to. What might those months have offered her? What else could she have done with her career?

She'd always wondered about these things, but had never fallen on the side of regret. Michael had deserved at least a few months of her undivided attention. He actually deserved much more than that but she knew that even in the afterlife, there's no way he would have expected her to ditch her work for too long. He would have known that it would have taken some work for her to properly grieve—and that work had meant literally working at the bureau for as long as she had been emotionally capable after his death.

She was relieved to find as she drew closer to DC that she was not feeling as if she was betraying Michael. She did personally believe that death was not the end; she didn't know if that meant Heaven was real or if reincarnation was possible and quite frankly she was okay with not knowing. But she did know that wherever Michael might be, he'd be happy that she was heading back to DC—even if it was to be severely reprimanded.

If anything, he was probably having a laugh at her expense.

This made Kate smile in spite of herself. She cut the podcast off and focused on the road, her own thoughts, and how even if she'd screwed up, life somehow always ended up seeming cyclical in nature.

***

She didn't get a rush of emotion when she stepped through the front doors and into the large lobby at the FBI headquarters. If anything, she was very aware that she felt she no longer belonged here—like a woman revisiting her old high school to find that the halls now made her feel sad rather than nostalgic.

The sense of familiarity helped, though. Despite feeling displaced, she also felt like she really hadn't been away that long after all. She walked through the lobby, checked in at the front, and headed for the elevators as if she had been here just last week. Even the enclosed space of the elevator was comforting as it carried her up to Assistant Director Duran's office.

When she stepped off the elevator and entered Duran's waiting area, she saw the same receptionist who had been behind the same desk a little over a year ago. They had never really been on a first-name basis, but the receptionist got up from her desk and rushed to hug her.

"Kate! It's so good to see you!"

Thankfully, the receptionist's name came back to her just the right moment. "You, too, Dana," Kate said.

"I didn't think you'd do well with retirement," Dana joked.

"Yeah, it's sort of a big snore."

"Well, go ahead and go on in," Dana said. "He's waiting for you."

Kate knocked on the closed office door. She found that even the somewhat gruff response she got from the other side made her feel at ease.

"It's open," the voice of Assistant Director Vince Duran said.

Kate opened the door and stepped inside. She had been fully prepared to see Duran and had readied herself for it. What she had not been expecting, however, was the face of her old partner. Logan Nash smiled at her right away, getting up from one of the chairs in front of Duran's desk.

Duran seemed to look aside for a moment to allow the reunion. Kate and Logan Nash met at the visitor's chairs in a friendly embrace. She had worked with Logan for the last eight years of her career. He was ten years younger than she was but had been well on his way to piecing together an illustrious career for himself when she had left.

"It's good to see you, Kate," he said lightly into her ear as they hugged.

"You, too," she said. Her heart swelled and slowly, almost teasingly, she realized that no matter how she tried to paint it, she *had* dearly missed this part of her life over the past year.

When the embrace broke, they both awkwardly took their seats in front of Duran. During their time together as partners, they had sat in this exact same place numerous times. But it had never been for matters of discipline.

Vince Duran took a very deep breath and sighed it out. Kate could not yet tell just how upset he was.

"So, let's not dance around it," Duran said. "Kate, you know why you're here. And I have assured Chief Budd that I would handle the situation in a very effective way. He seemed fine with that and I am fairly certain the entire ordeal with you tossing a suspect from his front porch will be swept under the rug. What I would like to know, though, is how you even came to be on that poor man's front porch."

She knew then that whatever harsh conversation she had been expecting was not going to happen. Duran was a monster of a man, roughly two hundred and forty pounds and the majority of that was nothing but muscle. He'd spent some time in Afghanistan in his early twenties and although she had never learned all he had done over there, the rumors were rampant. He had seen and done some harsh things and it often showed in the lines of his face. But today, he seemed to be in a good mood. She wondered if it was because he was no longer speaking to her as someone who worked under him. It almost felt more like catching up with an old friend.

That made it easy for her to tell him about the murder of Julie Hicks—the daughter of her good friend Deb Meade. She walked through speaking with them at a visitation at the Meade house and how certain the Meades had seemed. She then replayed the scene on Neilbolt's porch, explaining how she had started off by defending herself and then admittedly taking things perhaps a step too far.

On a few occasions, she got a soft chuckle from Logan. Duran, meanwhile, remained mostly expressionless. When she was done, she waited for his reaction and was confused when all she got out of him was a shrug.

"Look…as far as I'm concerned," he said, "it's a non-issue. While you *might* have been sticking your nose where it didn't belong, this guy had no business putting his hands on you—especially after you told him that you were former FBI. That was stupid on his part. The only thing I'd raise an eyebrow over is you slapping the cuffs on him."

"As I said…I admittedly went a little overboard."

"You?" Logan asked in mock surprise. "No!"

"What do you know about the case?" Duran asked.

"Just that she was killed in her home while her husband was away on business. The ex-boyfriend was the only real lead and the cops dismissed him in pretty quick fashion. I did find out later that his alibi was airtight, though."

"Nothing else?" Duran asked.

"Nothing that I've been told."

Duran nodded and then managed a cordial smile. "So aside from pitching grown men from their porches, how has retirement been treating you?"

"Like hell," she admitted. "It was great for the first few weeks but it got old fast. I miss my job. I've taken to reading an insane amount of true crime books. I'm watching far too many crime shows on the Biography Channel."

"You'd be surprised how often we hear that from agents in their first six to twelve months after retirement. Some of them call begging for some sort of work. Anything we have. Even paperwork of bullshit wiretaps."

Kate said nothing but nodded to indicate that she could identify.

"But yet you didn't call," Duran said. "If I'm being honest, I expected you to. I didn't think you could just drop it so easily. And this little incident proves me right."

"With all due respect," Kate said, "did you call me down here to slap me on the wrist over this or to rub my nose in how I can't outgrow my old job?"

"Neither," Duran said. "I was looking through your files yesterday after I got the call from Richmond. I noticed that you've been asked to testify at a parole hearing. Is that correct?"

"It is. It's for the Mueller case. Double homicide."

"Is it the first time you've been contacted about work since you retired?"

"No," she said, pretty sure he already knew the answer. "I had an assistant to an agent call me about two months after I retired to ask questions about a cold case I last worked on back in 2005. Some of the guys in records and research have reached out a few times about my methodology on some older cases, too."

Duran nodded and reclined back in his chair a bit. "You should also know that we have instructors at the academy using some of your earlier casework as examples for coursework. You left your mark here in the bureau, Agent Wise. And honestly, I was rather *hoping* you'd be one of those agents who started calling up to see what you could do to help even after you had retired."

"Are you saying you want me to start assisting with some cases, then?" Kate asked. She did her best to keep the hopeful tone out of her voice.

"Well, it's not that cut and dried. We were thinking of perhaps bringing an agent or two with an exceptional track record to work on cold cases. Nothing long term or full time, mind you. And when we have discussed it, your name was the only one that kept coming up in unison. Now, before you get too excited, please know that this is not an immediate thing. We still want you to relax. Take some time off. *Real* time off."

"I can do that," Kate said. "Thank you."

"Don't thank me yet," Duran said. "It could be a few months. And I'm afraid I'm going to have to revoke the offer if you go back home and start beating up men much younger than you on their porches."

"I think I can restrain myself," Kate said.

Again, Logan couldn't help but let out a little muffled laugh from beside her.

Duran seemed just as amused as he got to his feet.

"Now... if you truly are going to assist, I'm afraid we have to revisit one of the less spectacular parts of the job."

Assuming he meant paperwork, Kate sighed. "Forms? Documents?"

"Oh no, nothing like that," Duran said. "I've scheduled a meeting to get this going. Figured it would be the best way to keep all channels up to date."

"Ah, I hate meetings."

"Oh, I know," Duran said. "I remember. But hey... what better way to welcome you back?"

Logan chuckled beside her as they got to their feet and followed Duran out of the office. For Kate, it all seemed eerily familiar.

***

Really, it turned out not to be a bad meeting at all. There were only three other people waiting for them in the small conference room at the end of the hallway. Two of them were agents, one a male, the other female. As far as Kate could tell, she had met neither of them before. The third was a man who looked vaguely familiar; she was pretty sure his last name was Dunn. As Duran closed the door behind them, one of the agents got to his feet and instantly extended his hand.

"Agent Wise, I'm so pleased to meet you," he said.

She took his hand awkwardly and shook it. As she did, the agent seemed to realize that he had made a small spectacle of himself.

"Sorry," he said under his breath as he quickly returned to his seat.

"That's fine, Agent Rose," Duran said as he took a seat at the head of the table. "You aren't the first agent to be floored by the presence of near-legendary Agent Kate Wise." He said this with a bit of sarcasm and cut a thin smile Kate's way.

The man she thought was named Dunn stood out from the other two—both clearly younger agents. He was a supervisor of sorts; it was clear from his stoic expression to his finely pressed suit.

"Agent Wise," Duran said, "these two agents are Agent Rose and Agent DeMarco. They have been partners for about the last seven months, but only because myself and Assistant Director Dunn have had problems finding a place for them. They both come with their own set of unique strengths. And if you do end up taking the lead on this case in Richmond, one of them will likely be assigned to work with you."

Agent Rose still looked embarrassed but refused to break his concentration. Kate couldn't remember the last time someone had been so visibly shaken to meet her. It had been somewhere around the next-to-last year of her career when someone from Quantico had ended up working with her for a day in the labs. It was humbling but also a little off-putting.

"I should add," Assistant Director Dunn said, "that Deputy Director Duran and I are the ones that have pushed for this program to bring recently retired agents in. I don't know if he has told you yet, but your name was the first that came up."

"Yes," Duran agreed. "Needless to say, we'd really appreciate it if you kept it under wraps for now. And, of course, knock it out of the park."

"I'll try my best," Kate said. She was beginning to understand that there was now a bit of pressure being applied here. Not that she minded, really. She usually operated better under pressure.

"Great," Duran said. "For now, do you want to go over the details of this case as you understand them?"

Kate nodded and instantly fell back into her old role. It was as if she had never missed a day, much less a year. As she filled them in on what was going on in Richmond and how she had gotten involved, Agent Rose and Agent DeMarco held steady eye contact with her, perhaps studying her to see how they might work alongside her.

But she didn't let that distract her. As she went over the details of the case, she felt as if she had stepped back in time.

And it was far superior to the present she had been living.

CHAPTER SEVEN

Three hours later, Kate and Logan were sitting at an outdoor table beneath a canopy at a small Italian restaurant. Logan was eating a meat-packed sub while Kate was eating a pasta salad and enjoying a glass of white wine. She did not drink often and almost never before five in the afternoon, but this was a special occasion. Even the mere idea of a reality where she might once again become active within the bureau was cause for celebration as far as she was concerned.

"So what kind of cases are you working on right now?" Kate asked.

"All things that would bore you, I'm sure," he said. But she knew he'd tell her; he'd tell her because he loved the job just as much as she did.

"Trying to crack some scammers that have been tampering with ATMs for the most part. I'm sort of working in a partnership with a few other agents in what might be a small prostitution ring coming out of Georgetown, but that's about it."

"Yikes," Kate said.

"Told you. Boring."

"So a far cry from these cold cases Duran mentioned? What do you know about that anyway? How long has that little side project been cooking?"

"A while, I think. I was only brought in to the loop two weeks ago. Duran and some of the other behind-closed-door types were asking about some of the cases we had worked on that never got solved. Not looking for methodology or anything like that, just asking for details and old case files."

"And they didn't give you a reason?"

"No. And...wait, why do you sound suspicious? I thought you'd be jumping all over this opportunity."

"Oh, I plan to. But it makes me wonder if there is one particular cold case they are more interested in. *Something* had to have spurred on this sudden interest in cold cases. I seriously doubt it's just so Duran could find some way to bring me back."

"I don't know," Logan said. "You'd be surprised. You've been missed around here. Some of the newer agents still talk about you like you're some kind of mythological character."

32

She ignored the compliment, still stuck on her train of thought. "Also, why would he call me in only to send me back, telling me he wanted me to take some more time before starting? It makes me wonder if whatever the *real* reason behind it is might not quite be fleshed out just yet."

"Well, you know," Logan said. "Based on the way you're overthinking this whole thing, maybe he's right. Relax, Kate. Like he said…there are tons of retired agents who would die for this chance. So yeah, go back home. Relax. Do absolutely nothing."

"You know me well enough to know that's not how I am," she said. She took a sip from her wine, thinking that maybe he was right. Maybe she *should* just revel in the joy of coming back to work…sort of.

"Retirement didn't change that, huh?" Logan asked.

"No. If anything, it made it worse. I can't stand to sit still. I hate an idle brain. Cross word puzzles and knitting aren't going to cut it for me. Maybe deep down Duran knew that I'm too young to be put out to pasture."

Logan smiled and shook his head. "Yeah, but the grass in those pastures is pretty lush and green."

"Yeah, and there's cow shit everywhere."

Logan sighed as he took the final bite of his lunch. "Okay," he said. "Some of us need to get back to work."

"Cheap shot," she said, taking the last sip of her wine.

"So what are you going to do?" he asked. "Head back home?"

She honestly wasn't quite sure yet. Part of her wanted to stay in DC just for the hell of it. Maybe she'd get some shopping done or go out to her favorite spot at the National Mall and just sit to reflect. It was certainly a gorgeous day for it.

But then again, she wanted to be back home, too. While she had struck out in terms of Brian Neilbolt, the fact remained that *someone* had killed Julie Meade. And it seemed that the police were at a loss so far.

"I'm not sure," she said. "I may hang around town for a bit but I'll likely head back home before nightfall."

"If you change your mind, give me a call. It was really nice seeing you, Kate."

They paid their checks and left the table after a brief embrace. Even before Kate left, her mind seemed to have snagged on one particular thought, one that had come out of nowhere, it seemed.

Julie was killed in her home, while her husband was out of town. If there was a break-in of any kind, no one mentioned it to me. Not the police while I was being lectured, and not Debbie or Jim. If

33

there had been a break-in, you'd think that would have been mentioned.

It made her wonder…did the killer enter the house because he was invited? Or did they perhaps, at the very least, know where a spare key was hidden?

Those questions settled it. Once she'd given her glass of wine enough time to run its course, she was going to drive back to Richmond. She'd promised Assistant Director Duran that she would not beat anyone else up.

But she'd said nothing about not investigating.

Of course, the funeral was first. She'd pay her respects and do her very best to be there for Deb tomorrow. And after that, she'd step back into her role—perhaps with a bit more excitement than she cared to admit.

CHAPTER EIGHT

The next afternoon, Kate was standing in the back row of mourners as the Meade family and their closest friends assembled at the cemetery. She stood with her little breakfast crew—Clarissa and Jane dressed in black and looking genuinely heartbroken—who had managed to love on Debbie earlier in the morning. Debbie seemed to be doing much better than she had on the day she had asked Kate to look into the murder. She wept openly and let out a single anguished moan of sorrow, but she was still *present*. Jim, on the other hand, looked like a very broken man. A man who would go home and think long and hard about how sometimes, life just wasn't very fucking fair at all.

Kate couldn't help but think of her own daughter. She knew she'd have to call Melissa when the funeral was over. She hadn't known Julie Meade very well but based on conversations she'd had with Debbie, Kate assumed she had been around the same age as Melissa, give or take a few years.

She listened as the preacher went through the familiar Biblical passages. While her thoughts were very much with Debbie, they were also still slightly obsessing over how this could have happened. She had not come out and asked directly if there had been a break-in since she had gotten back from DC but she had kept her ears open. She had noticed that neither Jane nor Clarissa had ever mentioned a break-in, either. And that was odd because Clarissa somehow had a knack for knowing everything thanks to her nose for gossip.

She looked up at Debbie and Jim, noticing that there was a tall man standing by Jim. He was relatively young and dashing in a clean-cut sort of way. She lightly nudged Jane beside her and asked: "The tall guy next to Jim. Is that Julie's husband?"

"Yeah. Tyler is his name. They hadn't been married long. Less than a year, I think."

It occurred to Kate that maybe her little breakfast clique really didn't know one another very well after all. Sure, they knew all about their former jobs, favorite caffeinated beverages, and wishes and dreams for retirement. But they had never really gone much deeper. It had been sort of a mutual silent understanding. They had rarely talked about their families, keeping conversation surface level, fun, and entertaining.

There was nothing wrong with that, of course, but it left Kate knowing very little about the Meade family. All she knew was that Julie had been their only child…in the same way that Melissa was *her* only child. And while she and Melissa were not as intimately close as they had once been, it still hurt to even think about losing her.

Once the service was over and the crowd started to disperse in a tangle of hugs and awkward handshakes, Kate and her little coffee group follow suit. Kate, however, hung back where a few people had kind of hidden themselves away for a cigarette. While Kate was not smoking (she thought it a disgusting habit), she wanted to stay out of sight for a while. She scanned the crowd and found the tall figure of Tyler Hicks. He was speaking to an elderly couple, both of whom were openly weeping. Tyler, however, seemed to be doing his best to remain calm.

When the elderly couple left, Kate made her way toward him. Tyler was heading in the direction of a middle-aged woman and her two children, but Kate made a point to reach him first.

"Excuse me," she said, angling herself in front of him. "You're Tyler, right?"

"I am," he said. When he turned to face her, she could see the grief all over his face. He was drained, tired, and looked to be empty of just about everything. "Do I know you?"

"No, honestly," she said. "I'm a friend of Julie's mother, though. My name is Kate Wise."

A flicker of recognition sparkled in his eyes for a moment. It made his face look almost alive for a split second. "Yeah, I heard Debbie mention you. You're an FBI agent or something, right?"

"Well, recently retired. But yes, that's the gist of it."

"Sorry she sent you looking into what happened to Julie. I can imagine that made for an awkward situation."

"No need to apologize," Kate said. "I can't even imagine what she's been going through. But look…I'll make this quick. I won't want to take up too much of your time. I know that Debbie wanted me to look into the ex-boyfriend and while I haven't been able to speak with her about it yet, he *is* clean."

"Mrs. Wise, you don't have to do this for her."

"I know," she said. "But I was wondering if you could maybe answer a few really quick questions for me."

He looked insulted at first but then resigned himself. A curious and sad look crossed his face as he asked: "Do you think there are questions worth asking?"

"Perhaps."

"Then yes, I'll answer a few. Quickly, please."

"Of course. I was wondering if you had seen anything around the house once you returned home that might have seemed strange or out of place. Maybe something that didn't seem like that big of a deal considering what has just happened to Julie. Maybe something you thought you'd look into later, when things had calmed down a bit."

He shook his head slowly, looking back to the place where his wife would be lowered into the ground within the hour. "Not that I can think of."

"Not even any signs of a break-in?"

His attention went back to her and now he looked a little spooked. "You know, I've started to wonder about that myself," he said. "All of the doors were locked when I got home that next day. I rang the doorbell because my keys were in one of my bags and I didn't want to dig for them. But Julie never answered. I didn't even bother to think about that until yesterday, when I was trying to get to sleep. Someone came in easily, without breaking in. And then they locked the door behind them. So they *knew* how to get in. But that doesn't make sense."

"And why not?"

"Because there's a code for the security system that only Julie, myself, and our cleaning lady knows. We change it every two months."

"Any suspicion about the cleaning lady or her family?"

"Well, she's pushing sixty and we don't know her family. The police were looking into it but found nothing."

"Well, how about you?" Kate asked. "Is there anyone you can think of that would have even considered doing this?"

He shook his head without giving it much thought. "I've spent every waking moment since I came home and found her body trying to think of someone who would have any reason to kill her—to even be *angry* with her. And I keep coming up blank." He paused here and then looked at her skeptically. "You said you're retired. So why are you so interested in this case?"

She gave the only answer that would be acceptable. "I just wanted to do everything I could to ease Debbie's mind."

She knew that there was a deeper truth, though. And it was a selfish one.

Because being just a little involved in this case is the most purposeful I've felt since I retired a year ago.

"Well, I appreciate your help," Tyler said. "And if you need anything else from me, please let me know."

"I will," she said as she gave him a lame sympathetic clap on the back and left him to his sorrow. The truth was, though, that she doubted she'd ever speak to him again. She'd been an agent long enough to know an innocent and truly heartbroken man when she saw one. She'd bet everything she owned on the fact that Tyler Hicks had not killed his wife. She already felt terrible for hijacking him after his wife's funeral. She'd stay away from Tyler from this point on; if he could be of any further help, let the cops handle it.

She went to her car and pulled out into the slumbering line of traffic that was leaving the graveyard. She drove back toward her house in silence, her thoughts continually drifting to Melissa and her forthcoming granddaughter.

Her phone rang, obliterating the train of thought. There was a number, not a name, on the display screen. She answered it suspiciously, still shaken over the funeral and how the experience was making her think long and hard about her own daughter.

"Kate Wise?" a man on the other end asked.

"Yes, this is Kate," she said.

"This is Randall Budd. How are you?"

"Somber," she answered honestly, a little pissed that she was having to speak to Chief Budd in that particular moment.

"You go to the funeral today?" he asked.

She was rather surprised that he even knew Julie had been buried today. Maybe she should cut the guy some slack after all. "Yeah," she answered. "Just left about fifteen minutes ago."

"Well, look. I wanted to call to let you know that at about eight o'clock this morning, we got an anonymous tip. An arrest was made in the death of Julie Hicks. We've still got the guy here in interrogation. Some guy that came out to fix their Internet a few weeks back. He's got some intimate knowledge of the family *and* he has a previous arrest record for—get this—sexual misconduct. We're looking into his story and accounts and it all looks solid."

"Who is it?"

Budd sighed, a sound that was like static electricity through the phone. "Ms. Wise, you know I can't tell you that."

"Of course you can. I'll do nothing with the information other than try to help you."

"Yes, but with all due respect, I have not asked for your help."

"Can you at least tell me if the suspect knew the victim personally?"

The other end of the line was quiet for about three seconds, finally broken by a thick sigh and Budd's voice saying: "No."

She almost pushed harder but left it at that. If she really wanted to know, all she'd have to do was place a call to Logan. It would be a cheap thing to do but at least the option was there.

"And it's looking like he's the guy?"

"It's certainly a possibility," Budd said. "Once we have enough to book him for it, we're going to notify Debbie and Jim Meade. So please keep it to yourself for now. I just thought I'd do you the courtesy of knowing…in the hopes that you don't go all vigilante on us again."

"Thanks for that," she said. "Have a good day, Chief."

She hung up with a sense of relief. Case closed. That was a good thing. Now Debbie and Jim could maybe begin to start looking at what grieving was like with closure involved.

But then she thought about what Tyler Hicks had said about the security code. And even the things he had not said. About how someone would have to know how to get in unseen. How someone would have to know the family well enough to get inside the house after dark, past the security measures and locked doors.

By the time she got back to her house in Carytown, that relief was gone. If anything, it had morphed into an entirely new kind of certainty.

A certainty that told her that whoever killed Julie Hicks was still at large.

CHAPTER NINE

If there had been one aspect of being an agent that Kate had hated, it was the few times she'd had to appear in court to give her testimony or to testify against a prisoner's parole. However, doing it now, a year removed from her job with the prospect of returning in a minor role in the future, she found it exciting.

She was set to testify against a man named Patrick Ellis. She knew the history like the back of her hand but still hung on every word as the judge recounted the case for those in attendance.

"It has been proven beyond reasonable doubt that Mr. Ellis killed a married couple while they were hiking on the Blue Ridge Mountain trails in 1993. The married couple, the Muellers, had been discovered three days following their fateful hike. Both of their heads had been smashed in, the wife had been raped and sodomized, they'd been stripped naked, and disemboweled. During the initial case, the defense pushed hard for a ruling of insanity, given the gratuitous nature of Ellis's crimes.

"In the end, Ellis had been found to be of sound mind, having given far too much thought into the killings not to have planned it beforehand. Further evidence had shown that the Muellers had not been random; they lived just three streets away from him. He'd even mowed their grass for them one time when the Muellers were vacationing in Florida."

He paused and looked out to the courtroom, making sure it sank in. As he went over the minutes and notes from previous dates, Kate relived the case in her head. It had been twenty-five years ago but the case, like most of the ones that had taken her into a courtroom, seemed just as fresh as one that had occurred last week. Even Patrick Ellis looked pretty much the same with the exception of a ratty beard and a few gray hairs. He recognized her even before she was called up to testify. He gave her a smile that was just as sharp as a knife.

A knife I'm sure he'd be happy to plunge directly into my throat, she thought as she stepped up onto the stand.

"Before we begin," the judge said once he was done with catching everyone up, "I should make it clear to those in attendance that Ms. Kate Wise retired from the bureau a little over a year ago. Still, I have it on good authority that everyone she worked with,

40

including her superiors, gives her their full trust and confidence. That being said...Ms. Wise, I assume you know all of the reasons that are being given for the parole of Mr. Patrick Ellis, correct?"

"I do."

"Can you state those reasons for the court?"

"Of course, Your Honor. I know that during his first year in prison, Ellis was involved in three fights, one of which nearly killed him. I also know that during his third year, he began to attempt to get permission to reach out to friends and family members of the Muellers under the reasoning that he wanted to apologize. When he could not get that permission, he attempted to commit suicide by hanging himself. Lastly, I know he has regularly been attending chapel and Bible studies, and that he has apparently given his life to Christ. For the past four years, he's apparently been a model inmate and, in the words of several guards, is the very definition of a changed man."

"That's exactly right," the judge said. "Based on those details, what is your opinion of the possibility of parole?"

"Well, Ellis was originally sentenced to life in prison. And while the option of parole was tacked on to that sentence, I vehemently fought it at the time. And I will continue to fight it now. I can't say if Ellis is a changed man now or not. But I *can* tell you that the things I saw at the crime scene when the bodies were discovered was the work of a man that enjoyed what he had done. I can also tell you some of the deranged things he said to my partner and I when he was under interrogation. I know there are members of the Muellers' family in attendance today, so I'd rather not go over the things Ellis said in private. But I will if I have to in order to make sure that he never sees another day of freedom."

She snuck a glance toward Ellis and saw that his grin was gone. He now looked like a man who was being haunted by some nameless ghost.

"Do you not consider his good behavior and changed ways a sign of turning himself around?"

"I don't think it matters," Kate said. "Parole would make him a free man. Yes, he'd have tests and restrictions galore, but he'd still be free. He'd have some semblance of a life back. The married couple I found disemboweled in the side of a mountain twenty-five years ago don't get that option. So no...I don't find Mr. Ellis's change of personality any reason to grant parole."

She saw the grim expression on the judge and the shocked silence that fell through the audience like a series of boulders from the sky. Yes, in the past she had hated this part of the job. But it had

41

come back quite naturally and as much as she hated to admit it, she felt incredible even under the evil glare of Patrick Ellis.

***

She was on her way out of the courthouse twenty minutes later, directly after it had been decided not to grant parole to Patrick Ellis. The discussions in the courtroom had brought back very vivid images of the murders. It was hard to understand that those kinds of scenes had made up her life at one point. Granted, the Muellers had been among the worst mutilated and abused bodies she'd seen in her career, but the number of bodies had kept piling up and somehow defining what she did.

It had taken her until retirement to understand that. For each case she broke or folded, there had usually been at least one dead body. She didn't dare ponder just how many she had seen or been around in her career. It was those kinds of details and numbers that, she thought, could dive a retired agent to the brink of insanity.

Kate did not have time to consider the thought much farther. She heard someone calling for her from behind as she made her way down the courthouse steps. She smiled when she realized how they were referring to her. Not as Ms. Wise.

"Agent Wise!"

She stopped and turned to see who would still refer to her as *agent*. She saw three people coming down the stairs to catch up with her. One of them looked vaguely familiar. Maybe one of the family members related to one of the Muellers.

"Can I help you?" she asked. "I'm Paul Mueller," the face she recognized said. "I'm Clark's dad. Clark was…"

"Yes, I remember," Kate said. And she did. Though when she thought of Clark Mueller, she saw the top of a head caved in with a rock and a small intestine hanging from a gash in his stomach.

"This is his best friend from college and his sister," Paul Mueller said, gesturing to the other two.

A brief round of introductions were made. It was all rather surreal to Kate. It was the kind of situation she'd tried her best to avoid when she'd been an active agent. But now she felt she owed some of her attention to these people—people who had lost loved ones a very long time ago and had found some peace and solace because she had managed to find the person who had taken away a large part of their lives.

42

"We just wanted to thank you for staying involved in all of this when you didn't have to," Paul Mueller said. "If that monster had gotten parole…I don't know what I would have done."

"It's my pleasure," she said. "Retired agents do this sort of thing all of the time."

"I'm sure they do," Paul said. "But you were always the one person involved in the mess that seemed to genuinely care. You wanted to catch Ellis, sure. But you had a good heart. I remember one night where you humored my wife when she fought through tears for close to an hour to tell you a meaningless story about Clark falling out of a tree when he was seven years old. You entertained her while every other policeman and agent in the house avoided her like the plague. That has always meant the world to me."

Kate, never the best at taking compliments, had no idea what to do with that. She decided to simply give him a warm smile. "As long as I'm alive, Patrick Ellis won't get parole," she said. "You have my word on that."

Paul gave her a hug, as did the college friend and sister. They split off and everyone went their separate ways. Kate headed to her car, trying to shake the memories of the Mueller case out of her head. As she did, she realized there was something that had been said during the hearing that had stuck in her head like a splinter. Something about how it had turned out that Patrick Ellis had not randomly selected the Muellers…that he had *known* them.

She thought of Julie Hicks and couldn't help but wonder.

The thought was still with her when she got into her car and headed home.

43

CHAPTER TEN

The last serious relationship Kate had ever been in had lasted three weeks. It had gone no farther than a single awkward kiss and a few dinners. After Michael had died, she had told herself she would never even date another man. But life had gotten lonely and she'd tried her best. She'd tried with four different men and each had failed. She'd been too hard on them, almost *looking* for some reason for it to fail. And if she could not find a reason, she made sure to drive them away.

It would be easier if she could tell herself she'd been pushing these men away subconsciously, but that had not been the case at all. No, she'd done it on purpose each and every time.

Because of that, Kate had gotten quite adept at eating alone. She didn't mind it at all, not even the pitying stares of the younger couples who sometimes looked to her as a warning of their future. There was something almost liberating about eating alone and besides that, it was a great way to sort her thoughts. She'd often gone to coffee shops or martini bars when she'd been an agent when she needed time to think. She'd never liked the silence of an office, and trying to work quietly at home was unnerving. But in the midst of the noise of everyday people coming and going in restaurants, it was easier for Kate to gather up all of her thoughts. It always had been. It was one of the curious little quirks that Michael had enjoyed about her—or so he had always said.

Currently, she was eating fish tacos and cilantro-lime rice. A bottle of Dos Equis sat by the plate, half empty. She was sitting at a small table near the back of the restaurant as the dinner rush started to fill the place on this busy Thursday night. She was eating her tacos and thinking about the Meade/Hicks case. She wondered how possible it would be for her to get inside the house. She was pretty sure Tyler Hicks would entertain the idea but she also knew that such a request would be in bad taste right now. She figured she'd need to wait a few weeks. And if she had any hope of figuring out if the killer was still at large, she didn't have that kind of time...especially when the cops thought they had their man.

And maybe they did. Who knew?

Her thoughts then turned to Michael. Ever since his murder, her thoughts had usually turned in his direction whenever she had trouble solving a case. Michael's murderer had never been caught, despite her own best efforts and innumerable man hours put in by a handful of other agents. As far as Kate could tell—and as far as she knew even to this very day—Michael's murder had been a random one. Maybe a mugging gone wrong or just some fucked up junkie wanting to feel the thrill of murder. There had simply not been enough evidence to suggest otherwise.

So his unsolvable murder usually popped into her head when it seemed that a case might be out of her grasp. This time, though—with Julie Hicks and her worried parents—Kate wasn't sure if it *was* out of her grasp. She couldn't help but wonder if she would have already cracked the case if she had the FBI's resources at her disposal.

Or, she thought as she took a drink from her beer, *maybe the cops are right. Maybe the guy Budd told me they got is the killer.*

She doubted it, though. She'd heard nothing from Debbie or Chief Budd. Budd might not extend another courtesy to tell her that they were now one hundred percent sure and had officially booked the suspect, but she was certain Debbie would have. And since she had not heard anything now, ten hours after Budd's call, she assumed that meant that their current suspect was not the slam dunk Budd had made him out to be.

She finished off her tacos and her beer. As she settled her check, she ran over a quick checklist of sorts in her head.

When can I see the crime scene for myself?

Where was Tyler visiting while on the road and why?

Did the cleaning lady even have reason to give the security code to someone else?

How reliable is the security system the Hicks had installed?

If she were still an active agent, these were the kinds of questions she would consider to be busy work. But as it was, it was all she had to go on for now. Until then, she could only wait for either Budd or Debbie to call her to confirm that they had indeed found Julie's killer.

But with every minute that passed, Kate expected less and less that she was going to get such a call.

***

Kate walked back to her house, just six blocks away from the place where had enjoyed her beer and fish tacos. Night had just fully fallen and the temperature was perfect. Not too hot but not too chilly as summer did its best to hang in there while fall came in to bully it away. She figured maybe she'd wrap up the night with a glass or two of wine out on the porch, listening to the traffic and the faraway crickets that seemed to think there might still be some forest left around the edges of Richmond.

Yet when she reached her house, she saw that there was already someone on the porch. The agent in her grew alarmed right away but within a full second, she knew she had no need to worry. The man sitting in the rocking chair on her porch was a friend of hers. More than a friend, she supposed. Of the men she'd attempted to date since Michael had died, the one currently in her rocking chair had been the only one she had kissed…the only one who had spent the night at her home.

His name was Allen Goldman and as far as men went, he was a decent one. He was no Michael Wise, but no one was. Allen was one year older than Kate and also on the brink of retiring from a job in advertising. But he had his own little side business, doing niche advertising for independent publishing houses. He was always good to talk to, had entertaining stories, and Kate was pretty sure he'd treat her nice if she let him. Allen had gone through a divorce about twelve years ago and rarely spoke of his wife or the time he spent with her—which made Kate a little uneasy.

He got up from the rocking chair when Kate came up the stairs. He looked a little embarrassed but also glad to see her.

"Sit back down," she said, waving him away. "How long have you been there?"

Allen looked at his watch and shrugged. "Maybe twenty minutes."

"How long would you have stayed?"

"I figured half an hour. A full hour at most."

She pulled over the empty decorative flower pot on the other side of the front door. She turned it upside down next to the rocking chair. Perching herself upon it, she sighed and took Allen's hand. He seemed to appreciate the gesture.

"So what's up, Allen?" she asked, a bit skeptical.

He had a thing for just dropping by. He did it because she had told them on their first date that she enjoyed the element of surprise in a man. The last time he had done it—about two months ago—he had ended up spending the night. They'd slept together and discussed why it was a bad idea the next morning. They'd had dinner a few times since then but nothing had ever really felt the same.

"I thought I'd come by to see how you were doing," he said. "We hadn't talked in about a week or so."

"I'm good," she said. "Just…it's been a weird day. A weird week, actually."

"You want to talk about it?"

She thought about it for a moment and found that she *did* want to talk about it. She surprised herself when she started telling him all about the funeral. More than that, she shared with him that Debbie Meade had asked her to do some digging. She ended her account with her trip to DC and the potential offer to start working on cold cases.

"You really miss it, don't you?" he asked.

"Most of the time," she said. "How did you know? Is it that obvious?"

He smiled and said, "It's in the questions you ask. The way you talk to people. It spooked me on our first date but I quickly came to enjoy it."

"Yeah, I was impressed it didn't scare you off."

"Speaking of dates," he said, "I was hoping to take you on another one sometime."

She almost made a joke about how he likely wanted more than just a date if he was showing up on her doorstep. Given what had happened the last time he'd showed up unannounced, it was easy to assume he was hoping to replicate those results.

"Maybe some other time," she said. "This whole thing with Debbie's daughter…and then the thought of maybe picking up some of my old work again…"

"Things are getting busy, huh?"

"Hopefully. There are lots of things about my past coming up these last few days. I even had to testify against this real creep in court. A guy I put away in the nineties. Seeing his face and reliving the case…it was like stepping through a doorway into the past. It was weird. But…I sort of liked it."

"You know," Allen said, "I don't think I'd mind taking the back seat to your work."

"That's the problem," she said, kissing him softly on the cheek. "You're too good for that. You don't deserve the back seat."

He frowned and got up from the rocker again. This time, Kate did not tell him to sit back down. "So is that a no for now, or a no for the foreseeable future?"

"I don't know," she answered honestly. "Let's just say it's *for now* and see what happens later?"

"That's fair," he said, headed for the stairs.

"And Allen…call next time?"

He gave her a smile and a wave, and then walked down onto the sidewalk.

Kate watched him disappear from sight, down the hill until he disappeared behind the curb and in the darkness of the night.

He's a good guy, she thought. And she had no idea if she was speaking to herself or trying to convince Michael, wherever he might be.

Honestly, though, Michael would want her to date again. He'd want her to enjoy life to the fullest in his absence. So maybe it was just her. Maybe it was her once again trying to fill a hole in her life with work rather than the company of someone who cared about her.

It was another one of those things from that past that seemed as if it would just not go away.

CHAPTER ELEVEN

He was watching her when she picked her twelve-year-old daughter up from cheerleading practice. A month ago, it would have been swim practice. But summer was on its way out, so the pool was old news. Now football was on the horizon, as were cheer pyramids and pompoms. Kids these days...had to be involved in something. And the idiot parents were more than happy to keep them appeased.

He was parked on the far end of the football field. He watched her, squinting his eyes, able to make out the bob in her ponytail as she got out of the car and spoke to one of the other moms as their daughters chattered by the backs of the cars. After a while they parted ways and she started the car again,

When she pointed the car back out to the road, he did the same. He was on the other end of the parking lot, nearly fifty yards away. He watched her get onto the road, allowed two other cars in front of him, and then he pulled out as well.

It wasn't pursuit, not really. All the cars in the world could get between them and he'd know where she was going. It was Thursday. She and her daughter would stop by Subway on the way home. He wasn't sure what sub she got but the wrappers he'd seen in her trash had some sort of red sauce on them. Maybe a meatball sub.

When he passed by the plaza with the Subway ten minutes later, he pulled into the other end of the plaza. He parked in an empty spot in front of an Aldi's and watched the Subway until they came back out. The daughter was cute, but he wasn't into kiddy stuff. He guessed maybe he *could* be but he figured he had enough issues as it was. The fact that he had been following her for the better part of three months was proof of that. He'd followed her and studied her and these were the things he knew about her.

Her name was Lacy Thurmond. She was thirty-five years old. She was married to a man who claimed he had to work late on Monday and Thursday nights. But he had followed the husband, too. The work the husband was doing was in a motel room twenty miles away from the house, having sex with a girl who might be early twenties at most. Lacy Thurmond had an obnoxious laugh, a pet cat, a twelve-year-old daughter, and she liked to read. She worked from home, doing some sort of editing jobs for a telecommunications firm. She had at least two glasses of white wine or a couple shots of tequila every night. She and her husband had sex twice a week (though he had it four times, twice with the younger girl in the motel) and one of those days was always Sunday. The sex was usually rough and she rarely climaxed. When she did, she was very quiet and had to be on top.

He knew this because he had watched them on several occasions. They did not have a security system and because their only bedroom window faced the backyard, he could snoop and spy as much as he liked. It also helped that there was a kink in the blinds in the bedroom that allowed him to see in just fine.

He thought about those blinds as he watched them leave the Subway and get back on the road. He thought about something as mundane as a set of blinds, how married couples at some point had to agree on them and install them. It was both sad and comforting to him at the same time.

He allowed five cars between them between the Subway and their home—a distance of three and a half miles. He was driving by their house when she pushed the garage opener in their car and the door started sneaking its way open. He saw the empty space in the garage, the space her husband's truck would fill sometime around ten o'clock. One time he had gotten in as early at nine forty-five but it was usually ten or a little after.

He checked his watch. That meant he had a little more than three hours. If he had to, he'd kill the husband, too. But that wasn't what he wanted. He only wanted her.

But yeah, he'd kill the husband if there was no other choice.

But he really didn't want to hurt the girl.

Even *he* had to draw the line somewhere.

***

Lacy rushed through helping Olivia with her homework. There were some nights where she allowed herself to be a half-assed mom. Tonight, she was more worried about getting to that first shot of tequila than she was her daughter's homework. She'd had a miserable day at work and with the passing of each hour, she knew what the night was going to be like, making her feel stuck…making her feel like she couldn't care less if the day ended or not.

Olivia finished her homework as Lacy did her best to straighten up the house. She did a load of laundry and paid a few bills online while Olivia sulked on the couch with her iPhone, playing around on Snapchat.

As the clock wound down to 8:30, the night went as it usually did. Olivia said a half-hearted *goodnight* and retired to her room. Lacy knew she wouldn't go to sleep until around eleven, spending the rest of her time alone either drawing or reading. She was fine with this; she knew girls around the age of twelve or so started to distance themselves, spending lots of alone time in their rooms. Besides...Lacy counted herself lucky. She knew Olivia was a bookworm. She could be up there investigating porn or sexting some guy on her phone.

With Olivia in her room, Lacy allowed herself a few shots of tequila. It had never been her drink of choice but it *was* the drink that got her drunk the fastest. She'd been going to it a lot as of late, especially on Monday and Thursday nights. It helped her get through putting on a fake smile for her husband.

She knew what he did on Mondays and Thursdays. But she didn't know with *whom.* The dumb ass had used a credit card to pay for the room one time and he did a poor job of hiding the smell of perfume and sex. He *tried,* dousing himself in Axe body spray as if that in and of itself wasn't a clue as to why he came home late on Mondays and Thursdays.

So the tequila helped with that. She was usually pretty sloshed by the time he got home, making the conversation easier and making it simpler to slide into bed next to him when the lights went out, pretending that everything was just fine.

She sat at the kitchen table, taking several shots as she scrolled through his Facebook profile. She looked for any messages or comments from women she didn't know, anything that might be taken as flirting. But there was nothing incriminating.

It was nine thirty when she realized that if she didn't stop drinking now, she was going to get sick. She capped the tequila and placed it back in the cabinet. As she did, a very light knock came at the door. She found this odd and had she been of a sober mind, she might have been a little more scared rather than just curious.

She walked to the door, half of her heart expecting her husband to be there—maybe with flowers and champagne. Maybe he was going to tell her everything, to come clean and beg for her forgiveness.

She went to the door, trying to be as quiet as she possibly could as to not alert Olivia. Even as Lacy walked to the door, she could hear the light murmuring of whatever pop music garbage her daughter was listening to these days. It came from upstairs like a bored person whispering to themselves.

The knock came again just as she reached the door. She turned on the porch light and looked out through the trio of small square windows at the top of the door. The face she saw was not her husband's but it was a familiar one. Confused as to why she had a visitor so late, she opened the door. She wasn't afraid; she knew her visitor quite well. While he wasn't the nicest guy and, quite frankly, creeped her out at times, she thought he was mostly harmless. Also, being here at this hour, maybe something was wrong...

She opened the door and he stepped forward.

She did not even see the knife. All she saw was him making a hard slashing motion and then her neck felt like it had popped open. She tried to speak, to ask the question *What are you doing?*

But all that came out was blood. So much blood.

She stumbled back, falling to a knee, and then he was on her. And then the knife came down again and again.

Unable to draw breath and feeling the actual rush of blood from her body, Lacy turned her head toward the stairs.

Please God, let him stop with me. Please God...

And that plea to a God she had never really even believed in was the last coherent thought that raced through her mind as the knife came down again and her blood started to collect in a pool around her on her nicely polished hardwood floor.

CHAPTER TWELVE

One of the things Kate had not shared with her coffee community was the fact that she hadn't slept worth a damn since she had retired from the bureau. She'd originally had issues sleeping after Michael died but that had been more from getting used to having one side of the bed empty than anything else.

But after the bureau, the lack of sleep had come from a series of dreams and nightmares that had nearly made her afraid to sleep. Her doctor had prescribed some natural remedies that had worked for a while but had eventually tapered off. For a while, she'd relied on heavy-duty allergy medicine to knock her out cold, allowing her a peaceful night's rest here and there.

The thing about those sleepless nights, though, was that she could usually tell when they were coming. She'd feel something like a weight on her shoulders as the sun went down, followed by an anxiousness she could nearly touch and taste and feel.

She felt all of those things the night after the court hearing for parole concerning the Mueller case. She'd tried just ignoring it at first because it had been nearly two months since she'd had one of those nightmare-plagued nights. But when she settled down to bed, she knew what was going to happen; she knew what was coming. She could feel it almost like another presence in the room.

She thought about going to the medicine cabinet for a few shots of allergy medicine but decided against it. As stressful as the idea of the oncoming nightmares was, she also knew that they could, on occasion, help her to later analyze and structure her life. Also, as morbid as it may seem, they were usually an excuse to get a glimpse of Michael in something other than the few pictures and videos she had of him.

So she went to sleep, her thoughts chaotic as they were spread across thoughts of Michael, of Julie Hicks, of the Mueller case, of having recently met with Logan and Assistant Director Duran. Despite the knowledge that she would almost certainly be plagued with nightmares before the sun towed in a new day, Kate was able to find sleep almost right away.

And as it turned out, her hunch was dead on.

***

The dream started in a way it had not before. In it, she saw herself twenty-five years younger, scaling down the side of a small drop-off along the Blue Ridge Mountains. It was nearing noon and it was a gorgeous day. She knew the moment at once, knew that she was going to find the bodies of the newly married Muellers mutilated and gory at the bottom.

Only after Kate's feet descended the last few feet, holding tight to the nylon rope that was anchored about sixty feet above her head, the sun went dark and it was suddenly night. She found herself standing at the bottom of the drop-off. She looked up ahead and did not see the rest of the mountain. What she *did* see, though, was another person scaling down the side of the cliff face.

It was a man, dripping blood as he came. It splattered against the rocks directly beside Kate's foot. When the man got to the bottom, she saw that it was Michael. His face was distorted and bloody, over half of it covered by a black mass. And despite the gory state of him—the condition he had been in when his body had been found in the park—Kate found that she wanted to kiss him.

"It's all a wheel," Michael said. "It goes around and around. You either cling helplessly to it or you fall off and get crushed. A wheel…"

He crumbled to the ground and became dust, billowing out in all directions. And suddenly, Kate's subconscious mind understood that what she was experiencing was much worse than the typical nightmares she'd had in the past. This was something darker, something *deeper*…

She turned around in the direction of where she knew she would find the Muellers. When she had first been on the case, she'd been here with three other agents, a series of police, and a forensics team. But now there was just her, in the dark, knowing there were gruesome bodies somewhere along the dark rocky terrain.

"Hello?" she called into the darkness, not sure who she wanted to answer.

"Kate!"

A familiar voice very much like music came from the darkness ahead. There were looming shapes up there, the jagged edges of trees. Only, it appeared that some of them were moving.

"Who's there?" she asked.

Another figure stepped out of the darkness. A smiling man, waving at her in a way that reminded her of old footage from silent film, a disjointed and almost broken sort of motion.

54

It was her father. When he smiled at her a wave of panic, terror, and disgust rode up her back. He took a step toward her, his eyes shining white in the darkness. Without hesitation, Kate reached for her sidearm only to find that it wasn't there. She took a step away from him, feeling her heart shrink inside of her chest as, in one dreaming moment, she resorted to her nine-year-old self. She was terrified at the sight of him, of the dark around him, of the—

A hand reached out and grabbed her shoulder from behind.

She wheeled around and there were both of the Muellers, freshly killed with their blood still glistening. The wife's head was bludgeoned, resulting in a crooked and fragmented smile. Her very recent wedding band shone in the moonlight, the last sign of light Kate saw as the darkness closed in on her and swallowed her whole.

***

She woke up the next morning to start her daily routine. But rather than sliding out of bed right away like she usually did, she lay there for a few minutes, shaking off the cobwebs of last night's nightmare. She had not dreamed of her father in a very long time. Having him show up in her dreams so suddenly felt strangely like an invasion of privacy.

She took a moment as she sat up, looking at the three pictures hanging on her wall. One was of her during her second week as an agent, fresh off of her first arrest. It had been a drug bust, netting nearly one million dollars in cocaine. Her very first partner, a guy named Jimmy Parker, stood in the background with a smile.

That was back before shit got complicated and my career started to form a little history—almost like an urban legend.

She supposed that was why she was so drawn to it—why she wanted to go back so badly. If people were going to view her as a legend of sorts, she had something to live up to. Legends didn't just call it quits and live their days for chats over coffee or reading books on the back porch.

She looked sadly away from the picture of her and Jimmy Parker, fully aware that dwelling on the past could only make things worse.

She usually started her day off with a run through Carytown, or, if her ankles were giving her hell, she'd opt for the small treadmill in the basement. But she didn't feel up to it this morning, every ounce of her drained from the nightmare. When she finally did drag herself out of bed and started banging around in the kitchen for breakfast, she started to wonder why last night's

55

nightmare had been so powerful. Was it perhaps the stress of being asked by a friend to look into the death of her daughter? Was it revisiting a courtroom and having to come face to face with Patrick Ellis again?

She supposed it could be all of those things, all coming to a head and raising up her nightmares again.

But why my father? Kate wondered. *I let that part of my past go a long time ago.*

Just thinking about him as she fried up a few eggs made her feel immature and small. It made her feel that what Michael had said in the nightmare last night had been true. Life is like a wheel that you either cling to or fall from and get crushed. And one way or the other, it just keeps rolling on and on in an infinite loop.

As she sat down at the table with her eggs and a cup of coffee, her cell phone rang. When she saw that it was Debbie Meade, she answered it right away.

"Hey, Debbie," she answered. "How are you doing?"

"As well as anyone could expect, I suppose," Debbie said. "It feels surreal knowing that I can no longer make a phone call and Julie will be there on the other end. I tell you, Kate...I don't know how parents get through this when it's a younger kid—a kid that lives in their home, under their roof..."

Debbie trailed off here, as if distracted. Kate could hear a series of shaky breaths on the other line and decided it would be best to let Debbie take her time to collect her thoughts. She didn't want to seem pushy, even though it was Debbie who had called her and not the other way around.

"Look, Kate, I apologize if this is out of line, but I felt you should know something."

"What is it?"

"There was another murder sometime last night. Another woman, a little older than Julie but pretty close to the same age."

"Do you know where?" Kate asked.

"I do. And that's why I'm calling you. Kate...it was in the same neighborhood. A woman Julie knew pretty well."

"How did you find out?"

"There were police cars everywhere this morning. Clarissa somehow found out first and called to see if I had heard anything. This is...well, it has to be related, right? Same age range, same neighborhood..."

"It would seem that way," Kate admitted.

"Do you think you can get in on it?" Debbie asked. "I know it sounds stupid but knowing that someone I know would actually be looking into it…"

"No, I understand that. It's just…there are protocols in place, you know? The local police aren't exactly eager to hand over information."

"I figured as much," Debbie said. "Well, nonetheless, there you go. You at least have the information now. Do with it what you will."

Debbie attempted to insert a chuckle after this comment but it came out flat. She still sounded infinitely sad and at a loss of how to carry on.

"Thanks, Debbie," she said. "And please…let me know if I can do anything for you."

"I will."

But as they ended the call, the weariness in Debbie's voice made Kate think that she'd do no such thing. For the foreseeable future, Debbie Meade would be wallowing, sitting in the loss and trying to come to terms with it on her own.

And feeling his, Kate felt that she had to at least *try* to see what she could do.

Without any hesitation at all, she picked up her cell phone and placed a call.

CHAPTER THIRTEEN

It took three different calls, but Kate eventually got Duran on the phone. She was bounced back and forth between Logan, Duran's receptionist, and then, after ten minutes of waiting, a return call from Duran. She'd expected him to sound a little flustered and maybe annoyed that she was pestering him so soon after his offer of coming in on a part-time basis.

Surprisingly, though, he seemed happy to hear from her. "Look, Wise…I know you miss the work and you loved seeing me the other day, but let's give it some time, okay?"

"Don't flatter yourself," Kate said. "Look, I have a favor to ask. And maybe one that's going to piss you off."

She heard a sigh on his end of the line before he responded. "You already heard about the second murder, I take it?"

"I have," she said. "The mother of the woman that was killed four days ago told me. The location of this new murder and the age range of the women killed can't be a coincidence."

"Right as always," Duran said. "I have a couple of agents working with the State Police on it right now. I expect to have a pair of agents assigned to it by the end of the day. I think it's clear we have a serial on our hands and would love it if we could stop things before anyone else has to die."

"Likewise," Kate said. "Which brings me to my favor. I want you to temporarily reinstate me. Let me in on this one."

"Wise, I can't do that. It would be impractical."

"No, it would be impractical to not at least consider it. I live in the area. And it's not like this is coming out of left field. Two days ago we talked about having me come on as a part-time agent."

"Yes, to spend most of your time riding a desk and working on cold case files. Not to be an active agent out in the field. No offense, Wise but you're fifty-five years old."

"And you're fifty-eight. What the hell does that have to do with anything?"

"We discussed bringing you on for cold cases. This is not a cold case. You aren't trying to get greedy with my offer, are you?"

"No. I'll be honest. This one is right here in my backyard and a friend of mine is involved. So yes, I want it for selfish reasons.

There....that's my reasoning. Now what's yours for keeping me off of it?"

"You mean except for the fact that you've been out of practice for a year?" he asked.

"That's the best argument you have?" she asked.

She was glad she'd always had a mostly friendly relationship with Duran. She knew some directors who would practically behead their agents for speaking to them in such a way.

"Let me make some calls," Duran said. "I promise nothing, but I'll call you back in about an hour."

He didn't bother with a *goodbye.* He simply ended the call, leaving Kate to wait and wonder. Never one to just sit idly by, Kate finished up her breakfast and left the house. She got into her car and headed east, toward the subdivision of Amber Hills, where the two murders had taken place.

As she expected, there were police cars at all three entrances to the neighborhood. At the third entrance, she tried her luck at getting inside. As she pulled her car into the entrance, driving between two decorative pillars with the name AMBER HILLS emblazoned in gold trim on them, two officers stepped forward. Their cars were parked to the sides of the road, flashers twirling red and blue lights in the morning sun.

She gave the officers a little nod of salutation and entered the community. As she'd expected, there were a few looky-loos walking up and down the street. They were all looking to the south, down the same street Kate was driving down. She rounded a bend and saw several police cruisers parked in front of a two-story house that looked identical to most of the other houses on the street. An ambulance was also on the scene, but pulled to the side and not running; it was obvious that it would not be used for anything urgent.

She passed the scene and came to a T-intersection at the end of the street. She took a left, connecting back to the street that the Hickses lived on. She drove by their house, noticing that there were two cars in the driveway. One of them, she saw, was Debbie's. She wondered if she was currently in her daughter's house, collecting things to remember her by.

Kate made her way back out of Amber Hills and was five minutes back toward her house when her cell phone rang. Duran's name popped up on the display. She let it ring a few times before answering, not wanting to seem too anxious.

"Hello," she said, resisting the urge to answer with: *"This is Agent Wise."*

"Wise, here's the deal," Duran said. "I've had a conference call with the Section Chiefs and we came up with something that's a win-win for everyone involved."

"Sounds promising."

"We are going to grant you a temporary reinstatement," Duran said. "It will last for one month. In the course of that month, we expect you to crack the case down there in Richmond and to get your hands dirty in some of these cold cases I mentioned during your trip to DC. Based on your performance, that temporary reinstatement will be stretched out to a year. After that year, we'd keep you on staff as a consultant. Do you understand?"

"I do," Kate said, already excited about the prospects. She was, of course, hesitant. "How is that a win-win?" she asked. "What are you getting out of this?"

"Well, we'll be testing out something else during this initial month. We want you to work with a partner. This is a new partner, a young woman who quite frankly, has amazing potential. She reminds me of you in many ways."

"Sounds like a recipe for disaster, then," Kate quipped.

"Maybe," Duran said. "But she's not gelling with any partners. We think it might do her some good to work with you. Someone seasoned and with an amazing track record."

"I don't know," she said. "Why can't you just pair me with Logan?"

"Look, this is the stipulation. You either agree to the partner or I can't offer you the reinstatement. That's how it's going to have to go."

She was irritated but as far as Kate was concerned, it wasn't even a choice. If she had to serve as some ambitious young agent's mentor just to get in on this case, so be it. She figured she could have it wrapped in a day or two and then be done with the new agent.

"Agreed," Kate said. "Can you send me some information on this agent?"

"I can send you the basics via email," Duran said. "Do you still have your badge?"

"I do."

"Okay. I'll get your new ID and badge to you as soon as I can. In the meantime, use your old one. If anything arises, you can give local authorities my name and number but I'd really appreciate it if it didn't come to that. And one more thing, Wise."

"What's that?"

"I don't want you active on this case until your partner arrives. When you and I get off of this call, I'm making a call with a few other directors. Your partner will be on the way down to Richmond within a few hours. I know it's hard but I need you to hold off on being active on this until the end of the day. We have several other younger agents that could use this to cut their teeth on…and the last thing I want is to seem like I'm showing favoritism."

He was right. Knowing that she was in but had to wait several hours was like swallowing acid. But she also knew not to buck up against an opportunity like this. She had to be obedient, had to make sure she didn't cross any lines.

"I can do that. Which agent did you decide to go with? Rose or DeMarco?"

"Kristen DeMarco. I'll send you her details in a second. And Kate…I'm excited about this. I think everyone could come out a winner here. Play it right, would you?"

"I'm insulted that you'd assume otherwise."

Duran laughed on the other end of the line, a noise that Kate cut off by ending the call. But honestly, she wanted to laugh, too. Instead, she pushed the ball of excited nervousness she felt deep down into the pit of her stomach and headed back home with her hands itching to dig her old service weapon out of hiding.

CHAPTER FOURTEEN

As promised, Duran sent Kate an email less than five minutes after their phone conversation. Kate pored over it when she got back to her house and learned a great deal about her temporary partner. She did her best not to be too impressed but by the time she was done, Kate found that she was looking very forward to working with Kristen DeMarco.

She recalled briefly meeting DeMarco during her meeting with Duran and Nash back in DC. She'd seemed calm, collected and somewhat formal. But based on what she had read in DeMarco's dossier, Kate saw something else—something potentially special. So when the two women met at Amber Hills just after three o'clock that afternoon, Kate had high expectations.

As Kate got out of her car and walked across the street to the generic government sedan parked alongside the curb, she tried to remember DeMarco seeming so small. It would have been hard to judge as she had sat down at the conference room table, but DeMarco looked quite petite. Five foot five at most, and *maybe* one hundred and twenty pounds. Still, Kate knew it was not the appearance that mattered, but the drive and commitment to the job.

According to the records Duran had sent over, Kristen DeMarco had graduated at the top of her class from the University of Oxford, obtaining a Bachelor of Science in Psychology. She then went on to the FBI Training Academy in Quantico where she graduated with honors and absolutely rave reviews and comments from her instructors. She officially joined the FBI just over a year ago, coming in just as Kate had been on her way out. She'd spent most of that time in the Violent Crimes Unit until, without any real reason given, she requested to be released from that unit to work as a field agent not contained within one division.

All of that and DeMarco was only twenty-five. And despite that impressive background, the woman Kate saw stepping out of the bureau sedan looked like she was barely out of college. She was quite pretty, her blonde hair a bit beyond shoulder length. Her svelte shoulders sagged a bit, as if she were uncomfortable. She wore a dark navy blue top and a pair of pants that were somewhere between dress and casual. Her sidearm was not concealed at all, the holstered Glock clearly prominent on her little hip.

"Agent DeMarco," Kate said as the two women met. "Nice to see you again."

DeMarco shook her offered hand and gave her a quick smile. "Same here. It's a pleasure to be working with you. Any questions for me before we head inside?"

"What do you know about the scene?" Kate asked. "All I know is what the State Police offered and they were pretty miserable when they realized I had been given permission to work the case."

"Pretty cut and dried from what I understand," DeMarco said as they started walking toward the Thurmond residence. "The killer seems to have attacked right from the front door with a hard slash across the throat. Came inside and stabbed her at least six more times. Blood everywhere. Her daughter was upstairs the whole time but never knew a thing. The father came home around ten fifteen, screamed when he found the body, and alerted the daughter. That's all I know."

"Same here," Kate said as they walked up the lawn and toward the porch. "Let's see if we can find out some more."

As they made their way up the porch, two local policemen stood in the doorway to block their way. When Kate flashed her badge, the feeling was almost too good to believe. She felt slightly intoxicated for a moment but squashed it down, not wanting to allow it to go to her head. She watched as DeMarco did the same behind her and they then filed into the house.

They had to enter the house basically hugging the foyer wall. The entryway had been blocked off with crime scene tape, making sure no one stepped in the crimson mess that covered most of the foyer. The blood had dried but there was so much of it that it looked wet in some places. It was practically covering the floor. It had also sprayed up on the walls, one splatter reaching to about three feet high.

As Kate moved past the roped off area, another officer came walking out of the adjoining living room. It was Randall Budd. When the Chief saw Kate, he looked a little embarrassed. Rather than scolding her right away, though, he simply took a few more steps toward her with a flare of red in his cheeks.

I guess Duran already contacted him to let him know I'm on the case now, she thought. She was glad this was the case; it saved her an awkward conversation.

"Chief Budd," Kate said. "I'd like you to meet my partner, Kristen DeMarco."

Budd and DeMarco nodded politely to one another, their eyes both falling to the floor where the trail of blood tapered off just before it reached the carpeted area of the living room.

Budd looked back to Kate and gave her an apologetic kind of look. "I got a call from your director, so I know the deal," he said. "I won't get in your way if you can promise the same thing. I understand this is your case now but please extend us the courtesy of wrapping things up on our own terms as we transition it over to you."

"Of course," Kate said. "In the meantime, can you fill us in on what's already been done so we don't do any double work?"

"Well, we've dusted for prints and found nothing. Not on the body, not on the door, not the doorframe, nowhere within the foyer. We had a woman from the Department of Social Services come in to speak with the daughter and she's swearing that she saw nothing, and heard nothing. She had headphones on until she heard her dad screaming his head off when he found the body."

"And where's the father?" Kate asked.

"At the station. As of right now he's the only suspect. He was very confrontational when we started asking him questions. Half an hour in the interrogation room and he tells us that he was having an affair. He was coming home from meeting with the other woman last night. Got home and found his wife dead. The man is wrestling with some intense guilt."

"Does he know about Julie Hicks and how the two deaths might be related?" DeMarco asked.

"Not yet," Budd said. "I wish I had more to offer, but that's all we have. We've only had four officers working the scene, not wanting it to get too crowded. But we've got nothing so far. All we know is what the coroner's report is telling us. Lacy Thurmond was stabbed at least a dozen times, one of which was a particularly deep one straight across the throat. That seems to be the one that killed her. The others looked to be for the killer's pleasure more than anything else."

"Thanks, Chief," Kate said. "Let us know what we can do to help."

With that, Budd took his leave, slinking out of the door like a man who had just been dismissed from a case. Which, Kate figured, he sort of was. The two officers who had tried block the door from Kate and DeMarco filed out after him, leaving the two agents alone in the house.

They both looked down to the blood. Kate found herself also looking *up* at it, trying to judge just how far it had flown.

"Thoughts?" DeMarco asked. She asked in the vein of someone wanting to learn, not someone testing their superior. Not that Kate was her superior but regretfully the age difference made it feel that way to Kate.

"Several," Kate said. "I think the most important question is why Thurmond answered the door. To answer the door at that hour of the night, she would have likely known the killer."

"It could have been unlocked," DeMarco pointed out. "The killer could have simply walked right in."

"The fact that Thurmond was right here in the foyer, by the front door, indicates that she was answering the door. And I'd say all of the blood shows that the killer wasted no time. I doubt he was even invited in. The door opened and he attacked."

"Probably with the deep cut to the throat first," DeMarco pointed out. She then pointed to the walls. "Lying on her back, I don't care what artery you hit, blood isn't going to fly that high. Also, did you notice it was almost as if the killer *tried* to keep the mess in the foyer? There are only a few stray droplets on the living room carpet."

"Which means he's smart," Kate said. "He wanted to keep his chance of leaving any kind of clues or prints to a minimum. No prints on the door or the body also indicates that he was wearing gloves."

"Which means this murder was most likely premeditated."

Kate nodded, enjoying the back and forth. She was warming up to Kristen DeMarco rather quickly. "I'd also assume the husband is innocent. No reason for her husband to knock on the door. And if he admitted to an affair and he was with the mistress last night, it shouldn't be too hard to nail down an alibi."

They walked further into the house, finding it in immaculate order. The only mess to speak of was a pile of wadded up tissues on the coffee table and a little black book, opened up to the Ts. Kate saw the name of a few other Thurmonds and assumed the husband had made a few very difficult phone calls last night to inform family and friends of what had happened.

"Agent Wise, check this out," DeMarco said.

Kate had to admit…it was nice hearing those two words put together again. She walked into the kitchen where DeMarco was reaching into the sink. She pulled up a shot glass.

"It's the only dirty dish in the sink," DeMarco pointed out. She then sniffed it and wrinkled her nose. "Tequila."

"Maybe that's how the husband coped last night," Kate said.

"Or maybe it's how the wife was coping. Maybe she knew about the affair already. Men are typically pretty lazy about covering their tracks, especially if the affair has been an ongoing one."

They left the kitchen and looked around the remainder of the house. After twenty minutes of searching, they found nothing. Kate even checked the garbage just to be sure. In the trashcan in their pantry, she found nothing but discarded Subway litter and more dirty tissues.

"We need to speak to the husband," Kate said. "The daughter, too, if social services will allow it."

"I'll make the call," DeMarco said, already reaching for her phone.

Young, teachable, and super eager, Kate thought as they exited the Thurmond residence. *Yeah, I'm going to get along just fine with her.*

CHAPTER FIFTEEN

Kate was delighted to find that Chief Budd had meant what he said. The moment she and DeMarco got to the station, he stood aside and handed them the reins. There were just a few polite formalities and exchanges between the agents and the State Police before Kate and DeMarco were escorted to the interrogation room where Peter Thurmond was being held.

When they stepped inside, Thurmond looked up at them like a man coming right out of a dream. He looked half asleep and absolutely miserable. The sight of two women he hadn't yet seen since being brought into the station seemed to jar him a bit, though. That jarring became something more when Kate and DeMarco sat down across from him. Kate showed him her ID.

"I'm Agent Wise and this is Agent DeMarco, from the FBI," she said. "We've just come from your house and would like to ask you a few questions."

"Sure," Thurmond said, as if he really didn't care at all. "But I don't know if you can ask anything new that the cops haven't already asked."

"We want to get to the bottom of this as soon as possible, so we hope to be quick," Kate said. "First of all, was there anyone you or your wife knew who might have had any reason to come by your house so late at night?"

"No," Thurmond said. "I've been wondering that same thing myself."

"What about the woman you were seeing?" Kate asked. "Did she have a husband or boyfriend who might want to exact a skewed sort of revenge?"

"No. She's single."

"You're certain?" DeMarco asked skeptically.

"Positive," Thurmond said. "And by the way, I'm calling it off with her when this is all over. Lacy is dead because of the affair. If I would have been at home..."

"How about your daughter?" Kate asked. "Do you know if she had any young boys at school who were interested in her? I ask because the fact that someone murdered your wife but left your daughter untouched seems peculiar."

67

"None that I know of," Thurmond said. "You really think some teenage kid would be capable of something like this?"

"At this stage, we just have to make sure we're covering every possible base," DeMarco said. "Another thing to consider, Mr. Thurmond, is that the killer striking on that day, at that particular time, suggests that they *knew* you wouldn't be there. Was there anyone else who knew about the affair?"

"No one," Thurmond said. "If anyone, *maybe* the clerk at the motel. We used the same one every time and I think if he was really paying any attention, he might have figured it out."

"We understand that the police are currently holding you as the prime suspect," Kate said. "That's primarily because they can't find anyone else. So here's the deal: you've admitted to the affair. If you name the woman and allow us to contact her, you'll be cleared. All you need is that alibi."

Thurmond nodded, looking to the table between them. "Is there any way to do all of that without my daughter knowing? Without Lacy's parents knowing?"

"We can see to it," Kate said. "Of course, what the woman you've been seeing decides to do with this information is out of our hands."

There was a pen and a pad of paper on the table, presumably from where someone else had been in earlier, taking notes during the interrogations. Thurmond grabbed them both, scribbled down some information, and pushed it over to Kate. He pushed it away as if it were some disgusting, moldy meat. Kate looked it over and found the name of the mistress as well as her cell phone number.

"If the police are having problems with suspects, I think I know where you can start asking some questions," Thurmond said.

"Where might that be?" DeMarco asked.

"There's this tight-knit group of women in Amber Hills. Lacy was part of them. I'm pretty sure Julie Hicks was, too. At the risk of sounding insensitive, they're mostly made up of stay-at-home moms. A few of them aren't even moms…they're housewives. Nothing wrong with that, of course. But I always thought that whole group felt sort of like a clique. And as ashamed as I am to admit it, I can almost guarantee that they know more about Lacy's personal life than I do."

"So you mean to tell me that Julie Hicks and your wife were friends?" Kate asked.

"I suppose. I mean, they weren't like best friends or anything like that. But they hung in that same circle."

"Do you know the names of any the other women in that group?" DeMarco asked.

Thurmond gave a shaky smile and reached back out for the pad he had just handed to Kate. He took it and wrote on it for several seconds. When he slid it back over to her, he had added four more names.

"There are plenty more, but those are the only ones I know for sure. I figure they might be in danger if this guy is focusing on that group for some reason. And, like I said, they should be able to give you more information on Lacy than I can."

"Thank you," Kate said, getting to her feet.

"Mr. Thurmond, we'll check your alibi," DeMarco said. "Assuming she's cooperative, I don't see why you shouldn't be out of here soon."

Thurmond gave a nod of appreciation but his eyes again went down toward the table. He was more than just beaten and sad. He was ashamed.

Kate gave him a sorrowful look and took up the pad with the information he had given them. Once they were back outside, DeMarco instantly made the call to Thurmond's mistress while Kate sought out Chief Budd to request records on local citizens hoping to get the addresses to line up with the names of the other women Thurmond had given them.

And just like that, Kate was on the hunt again after a year on the sidelines.

CHAPER SIXTEEN

The drive back over to Amber Hills took longer than usual, as Kate and DeMarco hit the grinding stream of five o'clock traffic. People were rushing home from work and ambitious students who participated in after-school activities packed buses that all seemed to stagger traffic.

DeMarco took advantage of the situation, not letting the extended drive time sidetrack them.

"I guess now is as good a time as any to let you know that I did a little schoolgirl somersaults when I was told I was coming down here to partner with you," she said. "And somersaults are not something I do."

"That's much better than running away in terror, I suppose," Kate said.

"No, I mean it. Even when I was still in the academy, I heard stories about you. And then when I started at the Violent Crimes Unit at the bureau, I looked through a lot of your old files for pointers on how to break down a scene. I mean... you were the only one to get *anywhere* on the Paulson murders in 2005. And let's face it... getting out of that hostage situation alive in '89...they should make a movie about that! How many men did you have to kill to get away?"

"Agent DeMarco, that's not a very professional question," Kate said. But really, she didn't mind it. After a year in retirement, she needed the reminder of what she had once been.

What she still *was*.

"Sorry," DeMarco said. "I'm just honored to be working with you."

"That's flattering," Kate said. While she had received lots of praise throughout her career, this was different somehow. With DeMarco sitting right beside her in the car, it was more personal; she couldn't just brush the words of affirmation off with a shrug. "So it seems you already know quite a bit about me. What can you tell me about yourself?"

"Nothing worth noting. Grew up in a small town in Pennsylvania. Wanted out as soon as I could. When I was in tenth grade, one of my best friends was raped, killed, and placed on her front porch afterwards. No one ever found who did it. That made me quickly change my future plans of being a veterinarian, instead wanting to do something in law enforcement."

"Any reason you started out at the bureau with the Violent Crimes Unit?"

"No real reason on my part. It's apparently what I leaned towards in terms of abilities. It seemed like a good fit for a while."

"Do you mind me asking what happened?" Kate asked.

"I'm still not sure. This one case…it sort of just broke something in me. And it wasn't the blood or the gore—and there was a lot of it. It was a triple homicide and suicide. A father killed his wife, his ten-year-old daughter, and his six-year-old son before killing himself. Something at the scene just triggered something in me. You start to wonder just what the hell is wrong with people, you know? And sometimes you think on that for so long that you start to hate all humans. It makes you not want to be around anyone."

Kate did understand it. She'd felt it herself a few times earlier in her career. Sadly, there was no way to bear it other than to outgrow it. "So this case…are you going to be able to handle it?"

She cringed as the question came out. She noted DeMarco's slightly annoyed look, a look the younger agent tried to catch before it showed. But it came through, and Kate took note to choose her words more carefully from here on out.

"Yes," she said. "I don't think I would have been sent out here if that was even a question."

"Sorry," Kate said. "Bad choice of words."

DeMarco simply shrugged and looked out the window as they inched closer toward Amber Hills. Kate remained quiet after her little blunder. If the silence would be broken, she'd wait for DeMarco to do it again. She remembered what it was like to be a younger agent, tasked with working alongside someone more seasoned. You were always overthinking everything, even the words you said.

Kate felt for DeMarco, especially given that she had already opened up about such a personal part of her story. She wasn't sure she could have done it. It made her think about the nightmare she'd had last night, her father leering out of the darkness with a dark secret shackled to him, linking him to the darkness.

Kate quickly shook the thought away and focused on the traffic ahead that was, even then, just beginning to unclog.

***

71

Kate had arranged to meet with one woman from the circle of friends that Peter Thurmond had mentioned. Yet when they arrived at their destination, she was pleasantly surprised that there were two of them there.

The woman she'd planned to meet was Wendy Hudson. She lived just five houses down the street from Julie Hicks in a stunning two-story house that was one of the newer ones in the neighborhood. When Kate and DeMarco arrived, she answered the door holding a large glass of red wine. She was a striking woman, somewhere in her early to mid-thirties. It was apparent that she spent a lot of time at the gym and the tanning salon.

She led Kate and DeMarco into her dining room, where another woman sat at a large oak table. She also held onto a glass of red wine. And from the way her eyes narrowed and she seemed to make a point of sitting up a little too straight, Kate guessed it was nowhere near her first of the afternoon.

Wendy Hudson sat down next to the other woman and said, "This is Taylor Woodward. She and Lacy were best friends."

"Ever since middle school," Taylor said.

Kate guessed that on any other day, Taylor Woodward was just as pretty as Wendy Hudson. But the loss of her friend had apparently wrecked her. She looked tired, heartbroken, and about one more glass of wine away from being shit-faced drunk.

Kate made her own introductions as she and DeMarco took seats at the table. Kate gave DeMarco a little nod, letting her take the lead.

"We were wondering if there's anyone who might have something against your group of friends," DeMarco said. "We've got a killer not only striking the same neighborhood, but apparently the same circle of friends, too."

"I don't think we have any enemies that would resort to *killing,*" Wendy said. "Look…we know how it looks. We're housewives. And I know that a lot of people in the neighborhood look at us like those women that used to be on *Desperate Housewives.* We do all work, but it's either very few hours or just things we do from home. Lacy had her editing gigs. She made about two grand a month. But still…most of her time was free and we all spent it together."

"What sort of things did you do together?" DeMarco asked.

"Nothing exciting," Taylor slurred. "Shopping. Julie, Lacy, and myself sometimes go to the pool just to lounge around. And, even though I'm married, I honestly just like the attention from the few dads that end up having to take their kids."

Yeah, she's well on her way to being drunk, Kate thought.

"You mentioned some of you having jobs with minuscule hours," Kate said. "What other jobs besides Lacy's editing job are we talking about?"

"Well, Julie worked some part-time hours at this clean eating place," Wendy said. "Making smoothies and stuff. Maybe twelve hours a week."

"And did she work with anyone that she ever crossed?" DeMarco asked.

"Not that I know of," Wendy said.

"But you know," Taylor said, "Lacy used to work for a small marketing firm. She was one of the supervisors. One of the reasons she quit was because she said it was a toxic work environment."

"How long ago was this?" Kate asked.

"A year and a half, maybe," Taylor said. She followed this with a large gulp of her wine, her eyes wandering as if she was calculating the passage of time in her head.

"What was so toxic about it?" DeMarco asked.

Taylor shrugged, looking blankly into her glass of wine. Wendy frowned at her friend and then looked at the agents. "She never went into great detail about it, but there was a man there that apparently had issues with taking orders from a woman that was much younger than him. He called her names, started rumors about her, even one that claimed she had sex with him in the bathroom at work."

"And that's why she quit?"

"No, she quit because when she tried to fire him, the owner of the company sided with the man. When she left, she went to the media. No one really believed the story, though. The owner was a well-respected guy."

"Did she ever have contact with the man or the owner afterwards?" DeMarco asked.

"Not directly," Wendy said.

"But the asshole sent her dick pics a few times in the weeks after she left. Told her if he ever saw her again, he'd make the sex-in-the-bathroom thing much more than a rumor whether she liked it or not."

"And her husband never did anything about this?" DeMarco asked.

"No," Taylor said with a vicious laugh. "He was too busy fucking college girls on the side to care."

"Any chance you know the name of this man?" Kate asked.

"Daniel Seal," Taylor said, spitting the name out like venom.

"She's right," Wendy said, as if making sure the agents took the tip seriously despite the fact that Taylor was heavily inebriated. "He'd be a good one to check out. He actually used to go to the very same pool that Taylor mentioned earlier. Sort of a skeevy guy. Made no attempt to hide the fact that he was checking women out."

Kate glanced over toward DeMarco, every bit as pretty as the two younger women sitting at the table. If they were right about this guy, she couldn't wait to see how DeMarco handled him.

It made her think, however briefly, of tossing Brian Neilbolt off of his porch. With a thin smile, she looked at DeMarco and just like that, the tension that they'd felt in the car for a moment was obliterated and they were on the same page without speaking a single word between them.

CHAPTER SEVENTEEN

Kate had forgotten how spoiled the convenience of having the bureau's resources at her fingertips could make her feel. With just a single phone call, she was able to get the address and criminal record for Daniel Seal within ten minutes. He lived downtown, a trip that took about twenty minutes now that the afternoon rush had cleared off of the highways. Daniel Seal lived on a row of townhouses in a well-to-do neighborhood, everything standing at an equal height, and even the cars parked perfectly in front of the buildings.

As it turned out, they arrived just in time. As Kate and DeMarco were walking toward Seal's townhouse, he came out of the front door. He was dressed in a pair of gym shorts and a dry-fit T-shirt. He carried a small gym bag in his left hand, the handle of a racquetball racquet sticking out of the zipper.

"Excuse me," Kate said as they approached him. "Are you Daniel Seal?"

He looked both women up and down, saw the way they were dressed and the serious looks on their faces, and grew confused. "I am," he said. "Who's asking?"

"Agent Kate Wise, FBI," Kate said, flashing her ID and again relishing the familiar feel of the motion. "This is my partner, Agent DeMarco. We were hoping to ask you a few questions."

"Concerning what, exactly?" Daniel asked.

"About Lacy Thurmond," Kate said.

"Ah Jesus, this again? Is she going to ever let the past go? Look, I've talked to cops and lawyers and all sort of people about the little tiff we had at work a while back and—"

"Let me stop you right there before you put your foot in your mouth," Kate said. "We're here to ask you about your working relationship with her because she was killed last night. In her home, while her daughter was there."

The shock on his face was not of an emotional source, but of a stutter in his thoughts. He'd been so flustered about his past with her that the idea of her being murdered seemed to freeze his brain for a moment.

"She was killed?" he asked.

"Yes," DeMarco said. "And from what we've been able to gather, you had something of a toxic relationship with her."

"Yeah, like almost two years ago," Seal said. "You think because of all of that I killed her? You actually think I'm a suspect?"

"That's what we'd like to talk to you about," Kate said.

Daniel Seal vehemently shook his head. "No. Look, I'm sorry she was killed. Really, I am...she was good enough at heart, I guess. A bit of a bitch when she wanted to throw her power around as a supervisor, but a good enough person. But no...I'm not getting dragged into this. I'm not a killer. That's ridiculous."

He started to step away from them, heading in a diagonal direction across the parking lot. Kate went to step in front of him to block his way but DeMarco was already there. She moved quick, so fast yet casual that Kate barely even saw her do it.

"Where were you last night between nine and eleven?" DeMarco asked.

"At a concert," he said. "At the National. Jason Isbell was playing."

"You have proof of this?" Kate asked.

Seal was getting frustrated and doing very little to hide it. He dropped his gym bag on the sidewalk and pulled out his cell phone. He scrolled through some of his photos until he came to a video. He pressed Play and showed it to them. The video was a shaky hand-shot video of a concert. The audience was more audible than Jason Isbell, though.

"Still got the ticket stubs on my dresser if you need to see them," he said as he stopped the video and shoved his cell phone back into the bag.

"That won't be necessary," Kate said. She honestly hadn't expected Daniel Seal to be the killer anyway but to have it proven in such a concrete way so quickly was aggravating.

"We may call you later if her work history comes into question during the investigation," DeMarco added.

Furious, Seal picked up his bag and headed in the direction he had originally been walking. Kate watched him get into his car and slam the door. He hesitated for a while before cranking the car, perhaps letting the reality of what had just happened to him sink in.

"He seemed genuinely shocked," DeMarco said.

"Yeah, he did."

"That was enough for me to know it wasn't him. It's hard to fake that sort of shock. He's emotionally trying to hide the shock with being pissed at us."

Kate couldn't help but smirk. DeMarco knew her stuff, that was for sure. She probably also knew that a solid tell when speaking to a killer was that there was usually a split second of recognition and pride in a killer's face when confronted about their murders. Kate had seen not a single flicker of that from Daniel Seal.

"You a night owl, Agent DeMarco?" Kate asked.

"I happen to do my best thinking after the sun goes down."

"Same here," Kate said.

This was true, but it had been a while since she'd stayed up past eleven at night. On the few occasions she had in the last few months, it had been out of fear of having one of her nightmares.

"What are you thinking?" DeMarco asked.

"I'm thinking I'll buy the first round of coffee on the way to speak to the coroner."

"You think the police missed something?"

"Probably not," Kate said. "But I do know that even when dead, people can tell stories. Sometimes it's just harder to hear them talking. You have to really look hard to see what they're trying to tell you."

DeMarco smiled at the thought. Again, nothing verbal was exchanged between them as they headed back for their car with the night wide open ahead of them.

CHAPTER EIGHTEEN

Kate kept her word and paid for the first round of coffee just after seven thirty that evening. After visiting a drive-thru Starbucks, they headed for the morgue. This time it was Kate who made sure none of their time was passed in awkward silences. But instead of trying to pry more life details from DeMarco, she focused on the case at hand. She'd always relied on partners as a sounding board—a social way to think out loud and get real-time constructive feedback.

"After the coroner, I want to go back to the house. The killer was there at night. He knocked on the door when it was dark. I wonder if he just walked right up to the door."

"With the Julie Hicks case, there was evidence that the security panel outside had been tampered with. Someone poured water on it from what they could tell."

"I read that, too," Kate said. "So if it's the same killer, that fact shows that he knew the house well. It also meant he was in the yard. He was bold. It was like he knew the property well."

"Maybe he does," DeMarco offered. "Maybe he's even a local to the neighborhood. Maybe he lives in Amber Hills and just had enough of the stay-at-home mom clique. There was this case I worked my second year on the Violent Crimes Unit about this guy who raped three women that all belonged to the same pool. The guy had no connection to them; he worked for the snack company that filled the vending machines at the pool. When we busted him, he said he did it because he couldn't stand seeing them flaunt themselves around the pool. Said it drove him crazy and he just couldn't stop himself."

"It's a good direction to think down but seems like a bit of stretch at first glance," Kate said. "I'm leaning towards the train of thought that it's a killer who has chosen that particular neighborhood for some reason. *Maybe* for the same sort of reason your rapist did."

They spit-balled ideas back and forth for the next twenty minutes as Kate drove to the morgue. When they got there, Kate was not at all surprised to find that the effort put into Lacy Thurmond had been minimal. After all, the cut to the throat made the cause of death fairly clear.

Still, the coroner was more than willing to speak with them. He was a tall, lean man named Smith. The sort of gaunt figure you'd almost expect to work in a morgue or a funeral home. He took them to the body, laid out and prepared for the makeup artist to come in the following day to prep Lacy Thurmond for her funeral. The work to her throat was exceptional, though Kate imagined she'd need to be dressed in something with a high neck to truly cover it up.

"Any other findings at all?" Kate asked.

"Nothing," Smith said. "No bruising, not even any sign of a forceful shove. No sexual abuse, nothing."

"Any way to tell which stab wound came first?" Kate asked.

"I'm almost positive the cut to the neck came first," he answered. "It makes the most sense logistically."

Kate nodded, figuring that he was right. None of the other stab wounds would have incapacitated Lacy. One stab and she would have run. But one like that to the throat and you were basically done for right away.

"And do you recall the body of Julie Hicks from a few days ago?" Kate asked.

"Yes. Same thing there. A bunch of stab wounds, one directly to the heart. But no signs of an obvious struggle. There's a very good chance the same knife was used based on the shape and length of the entry points."

"Do you think we could see a copy of the report, including images of the wounds?"

"Absolutely," Smith said. "Physical or email?"

"Email is fine," Kate said. "We need to get going. But thank you for your time."

Smith nodded and covered Lacy Thurmond's body back up. Kate and DeMarco headed out of the examination room, walking down the hallway for the lobby.

"Tell me," Kate said. "How often have you made yourself wear the Violent Crimes hat ever since you left that department?"

"Once or twice," DeMarco answered.

"I'd like for you to dig it up and try to figure out why a man would kill two women of a similar age, similar body type, in the same neighborhood. No apparent sexual lure, no known history with the victims. Can you do that?"

"I've been trying ever since my drive from DC to Richmond," DeMarco said. "And that's just the thing…"

"What?" Kate asked.

"It doesn't make any sense."

Kate parked in front of the Thurmond home half an hour later. She'd learned through updated reports that the husband was still at the precinct, cleared of his charges but unwilling to return home. And who could blame him, really?

As Kate and DeMarco approached the house, it had the feel of a haunted house. It was quiet, eerie, its windows like eyes leering at anyone who passed by. Before entering the house, though, Kate and DeMarco made a circuit around the outside perimeter. It was, Kate assumed, the very same way the killer had seen it before knocking on the door.

As she had suspected, there was no sign of forced entry. In fact, the yard was meticulously cared for, right down to the perfect shapes of the shrubs around the back patio. As they made their way back around to the front, she tried to see the house through the eyes of not just a killer but perhaps someone who could not afford to live in such a neighborhood. It was certainly an upper-class neighborhood, but not an exclusive one. Kate felt certain that if she were to check the property values, the average price of a home in Amber Hills would be around half a million.

This train of thought at least made *some* sense. Jealousy, after all, could drive men to do some pretty extreme things.

They entered the Thurmond house for the second time that day. The blood had not yet been cleaned, having set into the floor almost like paint. There'd be no cleaning it out now; it would simply have to be replaced.

"What kinds of things are we looking for this time around?" DeMarco asked.

It made Kate feel even more comfortable with her to know that not only was she open to learning, but she was humble enough to ask questions. Most new agents would avoid asking questions at all costs, just to make it appear as if they had everything together.

"Well, if we can't find motive among the victim or the crime itself, I'm hoping to find some clues within the house. The police have already ascertained that nothing was broken or stolen from what they could tell. The husband will come in later to confirm this. But at a scene as cut and dried as this one, I like to try to see the place through the eyes of someone who came here with the intent of killing."

"You thinking maybe the hot-wife suburban lifestyle might be the motive?" DeMarco asked.

Kate *had* been thinking this but did not feel it with any certainty just yet. Still, she couldn't help but think that if Lacy Thurmond had known the man well enough to answer the door for him at such a late hour, she'd apparently known him fairly well. And maybe that meant he had been inside their house before. Maybe he even had a look around when he was inside after killing her—bypassing the daughter's room.

Thinking of the daughter, Kate looked back to DeMarco as they headed up the stairs to the second floor. "Do you mind placing a call to the Department of Social Services to see where the daughter is? Might do some good to speak with her."

"Sure," DeMarco said. The expression on her face made it clear that she did not appreciate the busy work but she was as diligent as ever, pulling the phone out right away.

As she started making the information request on the phone, Kate checked the first room she came to on the second floor. It was obviously the daughter's bedroom; it was apparent by the clothes crumpled on the floor, the selection of girl-targeted paperbacks on the small bookshelf, and the set of cheering pompoms thrown up on the desk. It wasn't a messy room per se but it was disorganized enough to make it next to impossible to tell if there had been any kind of a struggle. There was no reason to assume this, though, as the daughter had not been pursued at all.

Kate zoomed in on a picture sitting on the desk among schoolbooks and craft stuff. It was a picture of Lacy Thurmond and a pre-teen girl Kate assumed to be the daughter. They were standing on a pier by a lake and looked genuinely happy. Kate started to wonder what kind of mother Lacy had been. If this picture was any indication, the two had been close.

DeMarco stepped into the room from behind. "Just spoke with DSS," she said. "They say the daughter is being transported to her grandparents' in Greensboro, North Carolina. They're asking for at least twenty-four hours before anyone speaks with her."

"That's understandable," Kate said. And honestly, she wasn't sure they even needed to speak with the daughter. She believed everything the husband was saying and part of his story was that their daughter had been in her room the entire time. According to the daughter, she'd seen and heard nothing.

The two agents scoured the house for another twenty minutes. Meeting up back in the foyer where the bloodstains remained, they both wore disappointed expressions. There had been nothing of note, not even something that could be considered a *possible* clue.

81

They left the Thurmond residence, Kate noting the presence of a patrol car parked across the street. It was good strategy, the local PD apparently hoping the killer might come walking by as a way to relive the moment. She wondered if there was another patrol car parked across from the Hicks residence.

"Want to meet for coffee in the morning?" DeMarco asked as they got into the car. "Maybe revisit everything with fresh minds and a good night's sleep?"

Kate honestly hated to call it a night. She had at least a few more good hours in her but she also knew that DeMarco was right. They had no leads and no matter how hard they looked, they likely wouldn't. It made Kate wonder if maybe they *should* speak to the daughter. Maybe she'd know of a family friend they had somehow overlooked. Or maybe she'd even know some sort of secret about her mother that she'd helped to keep hidden.

"Sounds like a plan," Kate said.

As they pulled away, she thought about Debbie Meade, wondering how she was coping with the loss of her daughter. As she thought of her, some kind of mental alarm went off in the back of her head, some indication that she may have missed something somewhere. She dug at the notion for a moment but nothing came to her. Maybe, like DeMarco said, a night's rest would help her uncover it in the morning.

Kate drove out of Amber Hills, the case gnawing at her. She took note of the patrol car parked out of plain sight behind the large stone sign reading AMBER HILLS. One thing was for sure: if the killer did choose to strike in Amber Hills again, he'd be trapped with so many cops around. And even if Kate wasn't there for the arrest, that was fine. Something about this case seemed more dangerous than usual. And although it was technically her first case since unofficially being asked back into the bureau, she'd be perfectly fine if someone else wrapped it up before she did.

CHAPTER NINETEEN

The moment she took her shoes off back at home, Kate realized just how tired she truly was. She'd been running full tilt today and most of yesterday as well. It had been a while since she'd asked that much energy of her body and now, as a result, she was beginning to crash. She went directly to the shower and spent most of her time under the water simply soaking in the heat. She'd prided herself with staying in shape for the last year but had apparently not done as good as she thought she had. She was sore, she was tired, and the case was beginning to taunt her.

As soon as she toweled off and slipped into a shirt and a pair of jogging pants, she sat down at the kitchen table. While she was certainly exhausted, she knew she would not be able to sleep with the case nagging at her like this. And now, more than ever, she felt that she had to get results. She had to knock this one out of the park if she wanted to have another few years at the bureau. If that was a flop, the men who had been working with Duran on this experimental project would likely pull the plug. She might even lose her chance to work on some cold case files as Duran had promised.

She looked over the case files as midnight approached. The only thing she knew for sure was that neither of the murders had been a result of love or passion. Even if there were affairs involved, killers in that situation usually made it known why they were doing the killing. But this guy was striking quickly and leaving right away. It was almost like he was playing some terrible mortal prank on the victims.

All in the same neighborhood, she thought. *All very pretty women. Victim Number One had no kids. Victim Number Two had one daughter, twelve years old.*

Both victims married. Victim Number One had a husband who traveled a lot for work. Number Two had a husband who was actively cheating on her.

That's when Kate's mind turned back to the little alarm that had been blaring at her while leaving the Thurmond residence. She had been thinking about Debbie Meade, wondering how she was getting along after Julie's funeral. There was something Debbie had said to her not too long ago, something she had shared with Kate and the other ladies during one of their little coffee get-togethers…

The ringing of her cell phone interrupted her. It actually made her jump a bit. Given the late hour, she was expecting the call to be from DeMarco or even Duran. She'd missed the days of randomly receiving calls about a case in the early morning hours and wondered if anyone every *really* got used to it.

But neither of their names was on her caller display. Instead, it was a name that made her heart feel like it had dropped into her stomach.

Melissa.

Oh God, she thought, thinking of that perfectly round baby-stomach her daughter had been sporting the last time they'd seen one another. She answered it quickly. Melissa was not due for another five weeks, making Kate think that this call was going to be of the bad news variety.

"Lissa?" she asked. "What's wr—"

"Mom, I'm on the way to the hospital."

Lissa's voice was thin and worried—the exact opposite of how she usually sounded. Kate had not heard her daughter this scared in a very long time. It broke her heart. It also sent a flare of panic through her.

"What's wrong?" Kate asked.

"My water broke. I'm having contractions and I feel sick to my stomach. There's…there's some blood, too."

"How far are you from the hospital?"

"Terry's driving…a little too fast for my taste," Melissa said, raising her voice at the end to maybe give her husband, Terry, a clue. "But we're about ten minutes away. Mom…I'm not due for another five weeks. Is this…am I going to be okay?"

"Five weeks isn't too terrible," Kate said, not absolutely sure if this was truthful or not. "It's not ideal but it should be fine."

"Will you come?" Melissa asked.

"Of course," she said, biting back her tears so Melissa wouldn't hear them and get even more worked up. "I'll be there as soon as I can. Can I bring you anything?"

"No," Melissa said, her voice sharp and hitched. It made Kate think she might be going through another contraction in that very moment. "Just you. Thanks, Mom."

Kate opened her mouth to tell Melissa to be as calm as she could but Melissa ended the call. Kate sat there for a few seconds, looking at the phone. Her heart resumed its position in her chest and she could not dent the absolute joy that flushed through her.

It was really happening. It was happening five weeks earlier than expected, but she was going to be a grandmother. Sure, there were a few jokes about age that passed through her mind, especially with the case files in front of her, but she didn't care.

All she could think about in that moment was her daughter and the new life she was about to bring into the world. Smiling from ear to ear, Kate swept up all of the case files into a single pile, leaving them on her bed, and then ran for her shoes by the front door.

***

After getting information from the front desk, Kate took the elevator up to the mother-baby section of the hospital. She went to the nurses' desk, hoping to find which room Melissa had been admitted to. Maybe she'd get to see her before things got underway. She had no illusions about being in the room for the birth; that was a duty Melissa would give Terry—a duty Kate would gladly forfeit.

Yet as she reached the nurses' station, she heard rapid footfalls coming from down the hallway behind her. She turned and saw Terry approaching. He looked frazzled, at his wits' end. It made him look haunted because Terry Andrews always looked so confident and well put-together.

"Terry…"

"Mrs. Wise," he said, once again ignoring her order to call her Kate. "It's bad. They think it's bad. She's…"

"Terry, slow down," she said, feeling her own spikes of fear starting to sting.

"Something's wrong," Terry said, tears brimming in his eyes. "They don't know what yet. But they just took her back for an emergency C-section. Her water broke at home but we didn't see until we got here…"

"See what?" Kate asked.

"How much blood there was. She kept telling me something was wrong and I just didn't want to believe it."

Kate knew she'd have to be the strong one here. She had never seen Terry so shaken up. And God only knew what it would do to Melissa to see him in this state. So swallowing her own fears, Kate took Terry's hands and looked him in the eyes.

"You got her here safe and sound," she told him. "You did your job and you did it every well as far as I can tell. Now the rest is up to the doctors. Let's you and I go sit in the waiting room and let them work, okay?"

He nodded, still looking her in the eyes. And although he seemed calmer, he still would not budge until Kate pulled at his hands and led him into the waiting room. It wasn't until her face was turned away from him that Kate allowed a few of her own tears of fear and worry to spill down her face.

CHAPTER TWENTY

At 2:02 a.m., Michelle Elizabeth Andrews was born. She had a low birth weight and there was a scary moment of touch and go where the doctors thought they might lose her. But about half an hour after she had been removed from Melissa, she seemed to level out. And while she'd likely remain in the hospital for at least a week or so to make sure she was completely out of the woods, everything indicated that she was going to end up leaving the hospital as a healthy—albeit underweight—little baby girl.

Kate, Terry, and Terry's parents were all informed of this as they sat in a collected group within the waiting room at 2:55. The news did Kate's heart a world of good but her own thoughts instantly went to Melissa and her recovery.

"I'd like to see my daughter as soon as possible," Kate said.

"You can see her now if you like," the doctor said. "In fact, she's been asking for you. She's still a little woozy from the drugs, but you can see her if you like."

Kate wept the entire way down the hall. She'd spent the last two hours or so not knowing if there was something wrong with the baby, Melissa, or both. And now that she knew that both were fine *and* that she was a grandmother, she was overcome with a joy like she had only ever felt when Melissa was born. She tried to have her face wiped off and her emotions together when she stepped into Melissa's room but was pretty sure she'd done a terrible job.

Melissa was lying in bed, her head turning toward the door as it opened. She smiled at Kate and Kate returned it. Melissa looked beyond tired, incredibly frail, and almost unlike herself.

"Mom…"

Kate went to her, took her hand, and kissed her on the forehead. "You did so well," Kate said.

"Have you seen her yet?" Melissa asked.

"Not yet. The doctors say we need to wait a moment. It's driving Terry absolutely nuts. Speaking of which, I need to get out of here soon so he can see you. He's worried about you."

"I know. And I hope he understands, but I needed to see you first. I just kept thinking about Dad and how happy he'd be…and Jesus, I miss him so much, Mom."

"I do, too. But he'd be so proud of you. For surviving this ordeal *and* for giving him a granddaughter."

Melissa smiled. "I bet he would," she said. "I love you, Mom."

"I love you, too. Now...I can see by your eyes that you're fading..."

"Sure am," Melissa said with a crooked little grin. It looked like she was drunk.

"So I'm going to tell Terry to come in now. But I won't go anywhere until you're of a completely sound mine. After all...I'm going to need to hold that baby."

Melissa nodded and gave Kate's hand a squeeze. It was hard for Kate to let go but she knew she had to. She had always been good about stepping back to let her daughter live her life, never interfering in the marriage in any way. This was the hardest moment in that vein she'd ever lived through, but she made herself leave the room.

Terry was already at the door, stomping like a bull to get in. Kate nodded to him and he went in practically in a run.

Kate stood there for a moment, frozen in the hallway of a hospital at 3:05 in the morning, feeling her life change all around her.

I'm a grandmother, she thought with a smile. *A grandmother who just resumed a career with the FBI at fifty-five years of age.*

She had to bite her lip to keep the childlike laugh from bursting forth from her lips. Maybe if it wasn't three in the morning the thought would not have seemed so funny. But as it was, the thought pushed her back down the hallway in search of coffee, ready to face this new chapter in her life.

***

Kate dozed uncomfortably in a chair in the waiting room for a while, the coffee not doing its job. The only reason she woke up was because her phone buzzed at her. When she jerked awake in the chair, she saw that it somehow came to be 4:15 in the morning. She also saw that the buzzing of her phone was a text from Logan.

She grinned sleepily, remembering how he'd always been a night owl. She wondered if he suspected her phone was always on silent after a certain time or if he was purposefully trying to keep her on her toes now that she was back.

Just checking in, the text read. *Hope all is going well. Let me know if you need anything.*

She rubbed at her eyes and stood up from the chair. She saw Terry's parents on the other side of the waiting room. His mother was hunched over asleep in her chair while his father was reading something on his Kindle. Terry, however, was nowhere to be seen.

She walked over to Terry's parents. Mr. Andrews looked up from his Kindle and smiled sleepily at her.

"I was going to wake you," he said, "but didn't want to be premature. The doctors came about ten minutes ago. They've given Terry the clear to see his baby. He's going to come out and let us know when—or *if*, I guess I should say—we can."

"Thanks," Kate said.

"Feel weird to be a grandparent yet?" he asked.

"I honestly don't really even know. Maybe when I hold her…"

"Same here," he said. "Terry's sister has been pregnant twice but miscarried both times. So this is a very bittersweet moment. I feel like we've technically already been grandparents."

"And how did it feel?" Kate asked.

"Pretty amazing," Mr. Andrews said.

Again, Kate felt alarms in the back of her mind. Something he'd said reminded her of Debbie Meade again…and just like that, she knew she'd need to speak with Debbie as soon as she could.

She nearly headed for her chair, to get her phone and send a text to DeMarco. But just as she turned that way, she caught sight of Terry coming around the corner. He no longer looked tired and worried; he now looked proud and borderline euphoric.

"You guys want to see your granddaughter?"

Kate absolutely *did* want to see her granddaughter. She also wanted to get an update on Melissa.

So while the case was very much still front and center in her mind, the part of Kate that had retired gladly pushed her forward, her hands eager to hold her granddaughter for the first time.

CHAPTER TWENTY ONE

What the coffee had failed to do in terms of perking Kate up, holding her granddaughter for the first time had accomplished. Aside from her own child—Melissa, now twenty-six and very much her own woman—Kate had never been a "baby person." In fact, the idea of being around them scared her a bit.

But holding Michelle had seemed to open something within her while also closing a beautiful circle that had opened up when she'd given birth to Melissa twenty-six years ago. It was like seeing a ghost and welcoming it into her arms. She knew this was not Melissa in her arms but the feeling of it was the same. She had not expected such an emotional reaction from holding her first grandchild but in that moment, everything within Kate softened and gave itself over to the child.

She'd left the hospital at 7:15 with only two hours of sleep but with an energy like she'd never quite experienced before. The knowledge that she'd promised Melissa she'd be back that afternoon pushed her on. Melissa had fully understood, excited to hear that her mother had gotten involved in bureau work again despite her retirement.

She texted DeMarco, letting her know of everything that had happened the night before. She explained that it might be a very scattered day but she *did* have one idea to pursue.

After placing the text, she then placed a call to Debbie Meade. She hated to do it because, in her opinion, not enough time had passed since Julie's death for Debbie to get involved with the case in any way, but because Debbie kept coming to her mind, Kate thought it would be okay.

Debbie certainly seemed to be okay with the idea of meeting with her—not at a coffee shop like usual, though. She wasn't at all ready to go out in public as she was susceptible to sudden bouts of weeping that hit her out of nowhere. Instead, Debbie had invited her to her house for coffee. Kate agreed, volunteering to pick up donuts on the way.

When Debbie answered the door at eight o'clock, she looked awake and almost happy to see Kate. The house smelled of recently delivered flowers in the wake of Julie's death and freshly brewed coffee. Debbie led her into the kitchen, where they sat at the bar.

90

Debbie poured them both generous cups of coffee and for a moment, it was almost like simply visiting a friend.

"Debbie, I wanted to speak with you outside of the group," she said. "A while back, you shared something with us. Something personal…about an affair. I hate to ask you to go there so soon after everything that's happened but quite frankly, I don't know where else to go."

"You mean *my* affair?" Debbie asked, shame crossing her face.

"Yes. And if you don't feel it's appropriate…"

"No, it's fine," Debbie said. "I've told Jim about it and we worked through it. And really, I don't even know that I'd call it an affair. It was two times and then I called it off."

"Does the guy live around here?" Kate asked.

Debbie shook her head, sipping from her coffee and looking to the bar; her embarrassment made it hard to look Kate in the eyes. "He was in town on business. I met him when he came to where I worked. He was selling some kind of new insurance for the employees. But Kate…I don't see what this has to do with anything."

"Maybe nothing," Kate said. "But it has come out—and please keep this between you and me—that Lacy's husband was having an affair. He admitted to it. And…well, I find it hard to see how a woman like Lacy, who spent most of her time at home, wouldn't be aware of it."

Debbie gave a guilty grin. "There were rumors that Lacy was having her own fun on the side," she said. "I assume you're asking me about my own affair to get into the mindset of someone that could have one?"

"More or less," Kate said. "Plus, you and Clarissa seem to have a better handle on the news that goes around smaller circles. I didn't know if maybe you'd heard something."

"Well, I can basically guarantee you that Lacy knew about Peter's affair. Everyone else did. He did a shitty job of hiding it. And if Lacy knew and kept it quiet…well, I for one assumed that meant the rumors I'd heard about her were true."

"That she was having an affair," Kate said thoughtfully. "Any idea who it might have been with?"

"No. And Kate, I see where this is headed. I know what your next question is going to be, so I can go ahead and cut you off right there. Julie was not having an affair. She loved Tyler very much. When he was away on business, she usually spent most of her time here with me or with that little circle of friends she had."

Maybe, Kate thought. *But you just said yourself that Lacy, a member of that group, was likely involved in an affair. And that she hid it relatively well.*

"You understand that I have to at least check, though, right?" Kate asked.

"Absolutely."

Kate took another sip from her coffee and stood up from the bar. "Thanks for your time, Debbie. And thanks for understanding when I had to ask the hard questions."

"Hey, I asked for your help," Debbie said. "I appreciate you sticking with it."

Debbie walked her to the front door and they hugged briefly. Kate had never really had any friends outside of the bureau so to know that she and Debbie were still developing a closeness between them was nice.

Walking back to her car, Kate pulled out her cell phone. While she believed Debbie that Julie had not been involved in an affair, she thought there might still be something to the thread of unfaithfulness, something that would drive someone to kill these two women in such an uncaring and almost casual way.

She pulled up DeMarco's name and sent a text. *The name Peter Thurmond gave us is next on the list. The mistress. Let's pay her a visit. Meet me in half an hour?*

She got a response before she was even in her car. She smiled and read the message, glad to have a partner who was as prompt and motivated as she was. Logan, while an amazing agent, had not been the best at returning calls and texts. Having someone so responsive by her side was a breath of fresh air.

Can do, the response read. *Meet me at my motel?*

DeMarco provided the address and Kate wasted no time. It was only 8:20 in the morning. If things continued to progress this quickly for the remainder of the day, she'd be back at the hospital with her granddaughter in her arms by lunchtime.

CHAPTER TWENTY TWO

The name that Peter Thurmond had scrawled on a sheet of notepad paper in the interrogation room the day before was Crystal Bryant. He'd also provided a number, which Kate didn't bother using. She knew if she gave the woman time to prepare, she could come up with lies and stories that could waste their time. She'd rather catch her off guard—a sneaky and almost dishonest tactic considering that Crystal Bryant was not involved in the case.

Ever diligent, DeMarco had already called in for Bryant's address and other pertinent information. Part of that information was discovering that she worked as a nurse at a physical rehabilitation facility from 8:30 to 5:00 Monday through Friday. This knowledge allowed them to skip a home visit and head directly to her place of business.

The office was located at one of the city's busiest hospitals and the waiting room was packed. Kate didn't see the point in singling Crystal Bryant out, so she stayed as nondescript as possible. When she and DeMarco approached the receptionist window, they kept their badges and IDs hidden. When she spoke to the receptionist, Kate kept her voice soft.

"I need to speak with one of your nurses," Kate said. "Crystal Bryant."

The receptionist looked a little confused, looking back and forth between Kate and DeMarco. "Okay...do you have an appointment?"

"We don't," Kate said. "It's a private matter and rather urgent."

"Okay. Can I ask who's looking for her?"

"No. Again...it's private."

Clearly unhappy with that response, the receptionist got up anyway. She walked away from the desk and disappeared down a hallway on the other side of the glass. Kate and DeMarco stood there for a few moments until one of the doors in the waiting room opened up. A pretty blonde woman of perhaps twenty-five years of age came walking toward them. She was dressed in nearly pressed nurse scrubs and looked very confused.

"Are you the women looking for me?" she asked.

93

"Yes," Kate said quietly. "I'm Agent Wise and this is my partner, Agent DeMarco, with the FBI. We'd like to ask you some questions about the Thurmonds."

Crystal Bryant looked as if someone had slapped her across the face. She looked all around, even back into the waiting room, as if to see if anyone had overheard Kate.

"It won't take long," Kate said. "And if you cooperate by answering just a few questions, it can be done without anyone knowing who we are or why we're here. So can we speak with you for a few moments?"

"Sure," Crystal said, obviously taken off guard.

They found three chairs in the far corner of the waiting room and settled down. Before Kate could even start asking questions, Crystal was talking.

"I guess Lacy's death made Peter come clean, huh?" she asked.

"Yes," Kate said. "Have you spoken with him since Lacy's death?"

"No. He texted and told me what had happened. He told me in the same text that he was done…that he couldn't see me anymore. Look, please…is there any way to keep this quiet? I don't want this getting out and hurting his reputation, especially after what happened with Lacy."

"We won't be telling anyone. We need to speak with you solely to get a better understanding of what you knew about Lacy. Do you think there was any chance she knew about the affair and was maybe having her own on the side?"

Crystal considered this for a moment. "I never thought about that," she said. "But I don't think so. She really didn't strike me as the vengeful type."

"So you knew her?" DeMarco asked.

"Not well. We had a few mutual friends but Lacy and I never actually hung out or anything."

"So you don't know anything about her personal life?" Kate asked.

"Just the few things Peter would tell me."

"Like what?"

Crystal shrugged and it was clear that she was getting uncomfortable. It even looked like she might be on the verge of tears. "He'd complain about her. About how she never wanted to have sex anymore. About how all she cared about was their daughter. He said he felt like he was always second. But…I don't know. I never really believed it. I'm not stupid. I'm ten years younger than he is and was…aggressive, I guess. He was just telling me things to keep me going back to him."

"So you can't think of anyone who might have anything against either Peter or Lacy?"

"No. I didn't know either of them that well."

Kate sighed, frustrated. She had secretly suspected this would happen, though. She'd been forced to look into multiple affairs in the many cases she'd worked on during her career. And in nearly every single one of them, the members of the affair were mostly distant. Aside from sexual preferences and their schedules, they typically knew very little about one another—much less the other's spouse.

"Well, thanks for your time," Kate said.

"Sure. How is he? Peter, I mean. Have you spoken with him?"

"He's grieving," DeMarco said. "And if he's asked you to please respect his wishes to no longer see one another, please do so."

Crystal seemed a little surprised to hear such a direct line of advice, but she nodded as she stood up and headed back to work. Kate and DeMarco also took their leave and as they walked back outside into a morning that looked to be thinking about rain, Kate's mind started to filter backward. This whole business with affairs was pinging some memory in the back of her head, one that she could almost pluck out and bring forward. But her head was too burdened with this new case, leaving her grasping at straws.

Some other case, she thought. *Something almost similar to this.*

"Hey, would you mind driving?" Kate said. "I need to make a call."

"Sure," DeMarco said as Kate tossed the keys her way. "Where are we headed?"

"I don't know just yet. Let's start with the closest Starbucks. I forgot how taxing these long days can be."

She cringed when she realized how old that comment made her sound. She got into the car and as DeMarco started the engine, Kate took out her phone and placed a call. When the warm and familiar voice on the other end answered, it was like being thrown backward in time.

"Wise, is it really you?" Logan asked with an edge of sarcasm.

"Yes, it's me. Thanks for your text, checking in on me. It was sweet…but unnecessary."

"Well, I was raised properly. I was taught to take care of my elders."

"Go to hell."

"With you, anytime. What's up, Wise?"

She couldn't help but smile. God, she had missed the back and forth she and Logan had established over their years of working together.

"I'm trying to recall a case," she said. "I'm thinking it's no older than ten years. There were two or three people killed because of some sort of swingers' party. An affair that came out of it and caused a lot of trouble."

"Yeah, I remember that one. What do you need? I can pull the files and send you whatever you need to know. You seeing similarities in the one you're working on?"

"I don't know just yet. I'm hoping it might help me get on the right track, though. I'm trying to remember the killer...what his MO was, the sort of things he said in interrogation and at trial. That sort of thing."

"Give me a few hours and I'll send them to you. Anything else? You want me to come out there and go ahead and wrap this case for you? Seems to be a struggle for you."

"Nope, I'm good. Enjoy your nice comfortable office. And thanks for the assist."

She ended the call and saw that DeMarco was giving her an awed sort of smile. "How do you do that?" she asked.

"Do what?" Kate asked.

"Keep track of all of your old cases like that."

"I've got a pretty good memory. Not good enough, though. I should be able to remember the killer's name."

"From ten years ago? Really?"

"Yeah. Sometimes the harsher cases stick with you."

"Oh, don't I know it. Violent Crimes taught me that lesson pretty quickly. And another thing I've noticed about these cases...something I also learned from earlier in Violent Crimes. Nothing about these murders seems personal, nothing passionate. I heard you asking on the phone just now about a swingers' party and an affair. But in my experience, most murders that spring from passion or lust or even love tend to be grisly. The killer seems to make a point to let everyone know *why* he's done it."

"I'm thinking the same thing," Kate said. "But I also can't help but wonder if it might be something oriented around secrets. Affairs being kept secret...maybe the killer is reflecting that in his murders. Maybe he wants to show that he can be just as good at keeping a secret."

"Forgive me for asking," DeMarco said, "but is there any particular reason you feel so certain there's an affair at the core of this?"

"I don't…not necessarily. But the fact that both women were married to absentee husbands has to be scrutinized. And the fact that one of those husbands was admittedly part of an affair makes it seem likely."

"Good point," DeMarco said, nodding as she pulled into a Starbucks parking lot. "The absentee husband thing is good. I mean, the Hicks husband was absent by necessity. Part of his job, with all of the travel. But being absent because of an affair…"

"Yeah, it's both ends of the spectrum."

"So I guess we just need to figure out if either of those ends is going to yield any answers," DeMarco said.

Kate nodded her agreement, thinking of the empty shot glass in Lacy Thurmond's sink.

What was she drinking to numb? Kate wondered. *The knowledge of her husband's affair or something she was hiding herself?*

CHAPTER TWENTY THREE

Logan had told Kate it would take him a few hours to get results, but her phone was ringing less than an hour later. She and DeMarco were sitting in the records room of Chief Budd's station, scrutinizing the records from both the Hicks and the Thurmond cases. In both cases, new information was still coming in but none of it was helpful in establishing a trail to a killer.

"Hey, Logan," Kate said as she flipped through a copy of Julie Hicks's coroner report. "That was quick. Sure you didn't half ass it?"

"I'm positive," he said. "So here's some pretty great news for you. Not only do I have a transcript from the killer's interrogation sitting right here in front of me, but he's also currently in prison in Chesterfield. Which, I believe, is less than an hour away from you."

"Why'd they move him?" she asked. "Wasn't he placed in Lorton Correctional Complex in Fairfax?"

"He was indeed. But population problems and his apparent exceptional behavior had him moved to a less strict prison."

"Exceptional behavior?" Kate asked.

"I don't have those details here," Logan said. "But yeah, that's what I have. Anyway, you still need me to send you over the files I have on it? We have them digital so I can just email them."

"That'll be great," Kate said. "It'll give me something to read on the way to Chesterfield."

"Keep me posted on this," Logan said. "All jokes aside, Kate, I'm rooting for you on this. There are a lot of us back in here in Washington that are rooting for you, actually."

"That means a lot, Logan. Thanks."

With the call over and a clear next destination in mind, Kate started tidying up the piles of papers and files she had been looking through.

"Chesterfield, huh?" DeMarco asked.

"Yeah. No lead, but the killer from an old case that is sort of similar to this one is currently serving time there."

"Oh," DeMarco said. She seemed stalled, though, as if she was trying to understand the relevance of it. "By speaking to him and maybe understanding why he did the things he did, I hope to be able to maybe apply that mindset to our as-of-now faceless killer."

DeMarco smiled as she started gathering up her files, too. "Can you fill me in on that case on the way?"

"Of course," Kate said. She was again impressed with DeMarco's willingness to learn. She suddenly understood just how much sense it had made for Duran to send DeMarco down here to work with her. It was more than just training; it was testing DeMarco on a variety of things.

As far as Kate was concerned, she was passing every single test with flying colors. And Kate was very happy to be her guide along the way.

***

Kate spent the majority of the drive down to Chesterfield filling DeMarco in on the case. Because she did not fully remember every detail, she had DeMarco scroll through the information Logan had sent as she shared what she knew. It was yet another example of how well they worked together—Kate recounting the case while DeMarco filled in the gaps.

The case was ten years old and, as Kate had correctly remembered, had involved a swingers' party gone wrong. There were four couples involved, meeting once a month. These parties went on for seven months before a husband from one couple and a wife from another decided that they would rather be together with one another than with their respective spouses. The two jilted spouses pretended not to care and, oddly enough, the parties carried on for two more months. But that ninth party was the last one. The rejected husband, named Tate O'Brien, killed three of the members of the group, including his wife and her lover. O'Brien sat in the home they held the party in until the cops arrived, gladly admitted to the killings, and claimed he wished he'd "had the balls to kill everyone else in the house, too."

But he hadn't just killed the three people. He'd butchered them. He'd also apparently had sex with his wife after he'd killed her. And while the reports differed, it had appeared that O'Brien had broken his wife's lover's right leg with a hammer and made him watch as he killed her and then proceeded to have intercourse with her while she bled out.

"Jesus," DeMarco said. "I don't know that I'd say that was a crime of passion, but it was surely motivated by some strong feelings."

"True," Kate said. "And so far, it does not appear that our killer is acting on emotion. Or, if he is, he is hiding it well. But what interests me is the fact that in speaking about the murders, O'Brien was so casual about it. *Yeah, so what, I did it. And?* That sort of mentality. It's very similar to the approach our killer is taking."

"Yeah, sort of casual. Of course, he's not sitting around and just waiting for us to pluck him up, though."

Kate nodded, wondering if maybe she was grabbing at straws by going to visit O'Brien ten years after his crimes. But damn it, she had to check every avenue possible, especially when leads seemed nearly impossible to come by.

As they neared Chesterfield, Kate's mind went back to the court hearing just a few days ago. She pictured Patrick Ellis, aged but very much the same man. It had been like a ghost from her past had popped up to haunt her and without her permission to do so. She wondered if it would be the same when she came face to face with Tate O'Brien. She'd only been in his presence twice, as the case had been very simple. But she remembered the almost vacant look in his eyes, the ho-hum expression of a man who literally did not care about what he had done.

Logan said the reports indicated that O'Brien had changed. But Kate wondered. Deep down, could a man capable of that sort of malice ever really change at all?

***

There were no movie-like settings where Kate spoke to O'Brien through a glass partition. Instead, she and DeMarco were led through a side hallway at the front of the prison, which snaked around to the rear of the building. There, their guide left them in the company of an armed guard who stood by a large metal door. The guard opened the door for them and stood his ground by the doorway.

"Nice to see you back at work," the guard said.

It was an odd comment because Kate did not recall this guard's face. It was another of those moments when she had to remember that, like it or not, she had made quite a name for herself while working as an active agent.

"I'm here if you need me," the guard said without much expression.

Kate and DeMarco entered the room. There were only a few things inside the concrete and brick room: a battered and scarred metal table, four chairs, and Tate O'Brien. O'Brien sat on the opposite side of the table from where they stood. His left arm was cuffed to a small metal handle that had been bolted into the table. Other than that, he looked quite happy to have visitors.

Kate studied him as she made her way to the table. He had aged considerably, the ten years that had passed morphing him into a man who looked to have aged at least fifteen or twenty. She assumed this meant that the few years he'd spent in Fairfax lock-up before being moved here had been rough on him. He had grown his hair out; it was down past his shoulders, curled and rather oily looking. He'd also grown a very large beard that looked in very bad need of a trim.

"Do you happen to remember me?" Kate asked as she and DeMarco took the two seats closest to them.

O'Brien shook his head as he looked back and forth between the two agents. "Should I?" he asked.

"I was one of the agents that processed you," Kate said.

"Ah," O'Brien said with a chuckle. "That was quite a bit of time ago. I try to not look back into the past."

"Well, I'm afraid that's why I'm here," Kate said. "I was hoping to speak with you about what you did."

"And what for?" O'Brien asked. "That case is closed. I did it. No question. I admit it. At the time, I believe I *happily* admitted it."

"So you no longer admit it happily?" Kate asked.

"No," O'Brien said, shaking his head bitterly. "I've changed quite a bit over these last few years. I don't really even know the man who committed those murders anymore."

"I don't understand," DeMarco said. "Do you mean you've grown past that? That you've somehow distanced yourself from the acts?"

"You could say that," he said. "See, right before I was moved down here to Chesterfield, there was this man coming to Fairfax. He did this prison ministry thing, reading the Bible, teaching us about sin and salvation. I fought it like crazy but after about six months, Jesus got me. I gave my life to the Lord about three years ago. Been on the straight and narrow ever since. I've repented of my sins and Jesus has redeemed me. So yes...I no longer identify with the man that killed those people. I did it, yes. I can't escape that. But I'm free of my sin now and believe I've been redeemed."

Kate couldn't believe her luck. If O'Brien had legitimately changed to such an extent, he could be more helpful than she'd originally hoped. That was, if she played her cards right.

"I'm glad to hear that," Kate said. "We're currently working a case that we can't nail down any solid leads on. You came to my mind because the killings are sort of similar. Not a crime of lust or passion by any means, but it could be in that arena."

"And how can I help with that?" he asked. "I told you…that's not me anymore."

"All the better," Kate said. "If you have truly distanced yourself from the murder and no longer identify with the man you used to be, you should be able to clearly describe how you were thinking back then. Think of it as another person. Describe him to me. Describe what he was thinking when he killed those people."

For the first time since they'd entered the room, O'Brien looked unhappy. He took a deep sigh and nodded slowly. "It hurts to go back there. I do sometimes, just to remind myself that even though I'm forgiven, I still did those terrible things. It's not like watching a man. It's like watching a demon—a monster. But I can remember what I was thinking. It's really clear when I let myself go back."

"I know it's hard," Kate said, doing her best to seem sympathetic. "But it really could help us. Anything you can remember."

He would not look at them as she spoke. He looked to his right, to the blank wall along the other side of the room. He was ashamed. It made Kate think that O'Brien genuinely had experienced an awakening of some sort. Kate, while a believer in God, wasn't sure about the whole *giving my life to Jesus* thing. But O'Brien apparently believed it and it had changed him for the better.

"I remember thinking that if I killed them, it wouldn't be a big deal," he said. "She'd cheated on me but I'd allowed it. I mean, in those parties, I'd cheated on her, too. But to tell me she *loved* another man, it was painful. It hurt in a way thoughts of her having sex with him didn't. And something in me…something in me just went dark. I remember thinking if I killed her because I loved her, it wouldn't be as bad. But if I killed her because of the rage I felt, it would be this terrible, horrible act. And so that's what I told myself. I told myself I was killing her because I loved her—because we, together, had ruined our marriage but *she* had to be the one to die because she had let it affect her heart. At the time, I thought the sex and swinging was okay. It was fun and innocent because we both consented to it. But when there was emotion involved…well, it made it easier for me to kill them."

"So it was casual for you," Kate said. "You managed to convince yourself that killing her because it was an act of love—no matter how skewed—made it okay?"

"Yes."

102

"Is that why you were so casual about admitting to it? I remember speaking not only to you but to the police that were first on the scene. They said you admitted to it right away, almost as if you didn't see what the big deal was."

"That's right. And at the time, I honestly didn't."

"Had you ever thought about killing before?" DeMarco asked.

"I'd thought about it *plenty.* From an early age, I'd always thought about killing my stepmother. And the neighbor's dog. I actually almost went through with that when I was about sixteen."

"So you did it for love?" DeMarco asked. "All three people?"

"No. It was just my wife for love. It was out of rage for her lover. And that third one...if I'm being honest, I just got carried away. It was almost...*fun* by that point."

It looked like he was on the verge of tears and Kate wasn't sure how much more he'd be able to take. It was just as well, really. She was pretty sure she'd gotten everything she was going to get from him. And while it really didn't amount to much, it at least shone a light on the mindset of someone who had no problem with casual killing.

"You said you almost killed that dog when you were younger," DeMarco said. "Why the *almost?*"

Kate was pleasantly surprised. She had thought about asking the very same question but figured it might not even matter; it was a subject that could easily take them off topic. But for a rookie agent, it was a great tidbit to have picked up on.

"See, that was a *rage* one. That dog would always chase our cat. When our cat had kittens, the dog got to the litter. Ate all but one of them. I had this twenty-two rifle I used to hunt with and I went out on the back porch one day when it came around. I aimed at it, almost squeezed the trigger."

"Even then, did you realize it was a decision based on rage, not love?" DeMarco asked.

"You know, I never thought of it. But yes, that makes sense."

"Have you talked to other men here about it?" Kate asked.

"About the dog? Sure. And even about the difference between what I thought of killing out of love and rage. Because once I was washed of my sins, you realize that there is no such thing as killing for love. Not even if you were to kill an intruder that was threatening your family. Even in that case, *love* for your family isn't why you kill. It's self-preservation."

"So then how do you apply that to killing your wife and the rest of the spree?" Kate asked.

O'Brien gave this some thought and nodded, as if understanding for the first time. "I suppose that was self-preservation, too. This other man had caught my wife. I had to defend my honor, or my love for her."

"So are you of the opinion that any murder, particularly those with lust attached to it, could not be done out of what the killer sees as love? Do you think all killers try to place the blame there rather than on the rage?"

"Oh yes. I see that clearly now. No murder is ever out of an act of love—no matter how much the killer tells himself it is."

Kate thought of the little circle of friends and lovers around Amber Hills and tried to apply this principle. It was surprisingly easy. And even if O'Brien was spouting some religious nonsense, it was a principle she had never quite latched on to over the course of her career.

And it made a scary sort of sense, given the current case.

Whoever was doing the killing was in some way *attached* to the victims but likely held no truly deep affection.

"Mr. O'Brien, I do thank you for your time," Kate said as she got to her feet. "And I'm very glad to see that you've changed."

"I wish I could help you more," he said. "But honestly…it's like watching a different person when I pull up those memories. I can tell you this, though. Someone killing in such a way, without any care or passion to it…he doesn't care about sending a message. He's not trying to prove anything, I bet. And that would make him more dangerous, right?"

It was a good point, but Kate wasn't sure how accurate it was. True, it didn't seem like the killer was trying to send any sort of message, but the proximity of the murders and the fact that the women were part of the same circle of friends made Kate think he *was* trying to prove something.

But what?

Self-preservation, like O'Brien had indicated. Was the killer trying to protect himself? And if so, who was he afraid might hurt him?

CHAPTER TWENTY FOUR

"You buy all that Jesus stuff he was talking about?" DeMarco asked.

The question caught Kate off guard. It was very direct and was easily the most personal question that had been shared between the two of them so far. It was also a question that was not easy for Kate to answer.

"I don't know," she said, trying her best. "I don't mind telling you that I believe in God. But when you get into the Holy Spirit and a resurrected Jesus, I start to have some serious doubts. Why do you ask?"

DeMarco shrugged. "Because I don't. I never have. I have no doubt that people can truly change—even people like Tate O'Brien—but I don't think it's because they symbolically give their lives over to the spirit of some man that may have never even lived."

"But you agree that a killer can have some sort of a change of heart?" Kate asked.

"Absolutely."

"They say Jeffrey Dahmer became a born again Christian in prison," Kate said. "So I guess that's some pretty substantial proof."

"Yeah, and he was killed by inmates later. So it appears that the Jesus he gave his life to cared nothing for him."

Kate couldn't help but smirk. She could tell that DeMarco was not broaching the topic out of the need for an argument. She was genuinely feeling Kate out, trying to get her thoughts on what they had just heard from O'Brien and how it might relate to their killer.

"You know, I can't help but wonder," Kate said. "We've been trying to get information out of the remaining friends in their little clique. But if there were secrets about their lives—things like affairs, for instance—then there's no guarantee they'd come clean. But there have to be others in Amber Hills who know those women...and maybe don't like them. But just in a normal way...the way some neighbors just don't like the people that live next to them."

"So you think we need to speak to neighbors as impartial parties?" DeMarco asked.

"Well, as neighbors, they'd hardly be impartial. But yes. If we're going to get the truth about that circle of friends, we have to go elsewhere. The truth we get might be stretched a bit but it's better than secrets."

"So we're assuming that Taylor Woodward and Wendy Hudson were being dishonest?"

"Not at all. That's a dangerous assumption to make about anyone. But I do think there's a chance they'd want to protect the reputation of their friends if there was anything dirty on them."

"Worth a shot, I guess," DeMarco said.

"Don't tell me you're one of those people that assumes the best about everyone," Kate joked.

"I do when there is grief involved."

Kate nodded. She usually felt the same way. But in a small gated community where she knew for certain there had been one affair and perhaps at least one additional one, she felt that no one could really be trusted. Because grief was one thing…but shame was a totally different beast. It was much stronger and could, at times, make people behave irrationally.

***

Before revisiting Amber Hills, Kate dropped DeMarco off at her motel. She then kept her promise to Melissa, going back by the hospital. With both the mother and the baby cleared as healthy, she was allowed to go directly to the room. The scene was totally different than it had been in the morning. When she got to the room, Melissa was beaming, holding Michelle in a swaddle of blankets.

She was alone in the room, which surprised Kate. She had expected Terry to be with her, never leaving her side. He was a good man and Kate was very thankful that her daughter had ended up with him.

"How's it going?" Kate asked, walking proudly to the side of the bed.

"Good," Melissa said. "My abdomen is numb from the surgery but my nerves are so jittery that I don't even care."

"Nerves?"

"Adrenaline, I guess. And the suffocating worry that I'm going to be a terrible mother."

"Nonsense," Kate said. "How many books did you read about birth and parenting in the last nine months?"

"Pretty much all of them. Still…now that she's actually here, it's like nothing I read really even matters."

"It comes naturally," Kate said. "Trust me. Hey, where's Terry?"

"He went down to the cafeteria to see what they had. He's been nervous, too. He hasn't eaten since my water broke. He's still nervous about little Michelle, too. They're coming back to get her soon. She has to stay in the NICU for a few days. But they said I needed to see her. That she needs the time to bond."

"Sweetie, I'm sorry I had to leave earlier. This thing with the bureau...I wasn't expecting it and the case is just going absolutely nowhere."

"So retirement is treating you well, huh?"

"No. It treated me like crap. That's why I was so happy to go back. But the timing, with Michelle and everything, it's all off."

"Mom, I'm used to you having that jacked up schedule. I've been living with it all my life. It was a good model, you know?"

Kate shook her head and sat down on the edge of the bed. "Let's not go there, Lissa."

"Mom, it's going to happen. I didn't waste that time and those credits in college for nothing."

"Didn't I tell you enough horror stories to keep you away from the bureau?"

"You told plenty of stories. But I think your plan backfired."

Kate said nothing. Ever since Melissa had first expressed interest in following her mother's footsteps into the FBI at the age of fifteen, Kate had been terrified. Even after her father had been killed, she had not swerved. In fact, Kate was pretty sure the death of her father had pushed her even harder. It was why she had made the dean's list at Marquette University and why she had followed her mother's career so closely.

Kate had foolishly hoped that after having a child, Melissa might change her mind.

But why should it? It hadn't changed Kate's mind after giving birth to Melissa.

"We're not going to talk about that right now," Kate said. "Instead, why don't you tell me what that nursery is looking like?"

"Oh, friggin' adorable," Melissa said.

And just like that, the subject was changed. They both knew there was an unspoken sorrow between them, the fact that the grandfather would never meet this little bundle of joy. Kate had never come out and asked but she had always wondered if the name *Michelle* was a feminine approach to Michael, naming the baby after her late husband and Melissa's late father.

"I do want to say something to you, Mom," Melissa said. "I want to let you know that it's pretty bad ass that you're back at work. It suits you. You could be doing this when you're seventy and it would seem right, you know?"

"Thanks…I think."

"I look forward to the day when you can give me some tips of the trade," Melissa said with a sly smile.

"I told you, we aren't—"

"Lighten up, Mom. I couldn't resist."

Kate rolled her eyes, leaned forward, and kissed her daughter on the head. It was the first time she realized that there were three generations in the same room, huddled on the same bed. Something about it was incredibly moving but, as a mother and now a grandmother, a little intimidating, too.

Maybe because she knew that when she left here, she'd be back on the trail of a man who was killing women—women not much older than Melissa.

With a chill riding down her spine, Kate looked to her granddaughter and then to her daughter. And suddenly, her work seemed to take on a whole new meaning. She wouldn't be able to do this forever. And as much as they joked about it, one of these days Melissa would likely end up with a badge and a gun.

And what about little Michelle? Who was to say what the future held for her?

Kate knew she should get going; the case and DeMarco were waiting on her. But with those new thoughts bogging like dead weight in her head, she stayed just a little bit longer, enjoying the presence of family and a moment of peace.

CHAPTER TWENTY FIVE

It was 3:30 in the afternoon when Kate and DeMarco drove back into Amber Hills. The police cars were still parked at the front gates while a few others were parked at seemingly random spots all around the neighborhood. Their search for additional information from the neighbors of the victims was shortened when they discovered that the neighbor to the right of the Thurmonds was not home and the house on the left of their residence was for sale.

However, when they ventured over to Helmsdale Street, where the Hickses lived, they found the neighbor to the right at home. When DeMarco knocked on the door it was answered by a woman of about sixty or so. A tiny little dog yipped at their feet, a breed that Kate couldn't determine. Something small and fluffy and white.

"Can I help you?" the lady said, her tone wavering between pleasant cheer and suspicion.

Kate showed her badge, the motion like a second sense now. "I'm Agent Wise and this is Agent DeMarco. We're investigating the death of your neighbor, Julie Hicks. Would you happen to have a little bit of time to answer a few questions for me?"

The old woman's face lit up for a moment but she managed to rein it back. "Of course," she said. "Come in, come in."

Kate and DeMarco followed the woman through her foyer and into a nicely decorated living room. Right away, she introduced herself as Caroline Manners and asked if the agents would like some coffee or tea. When both declined, they took their seats—Kate and DeMarco on the plush couch while Caroline sat in a reading chair.

"As I'm sure you know," Kate said, "Julie Hicks was not the only one to lose her life recently."

"Yes, it's terrible," Caroline said. Her little dog had leaped up beside her, curling itself into her lap. "I heard about Lacy Thurmond. It's tragic, given the state of her life. I assume you knew about her husband's affair?"

"We discovered it, yes," Kate said. "But how did you know about it?"

"Good Lord," Caroline said with a boisterous laugh. "Just about everyone in the neighborhood knew about it. I don't know if she ever admitted to knowing about it, but there's no way Lacy *didn't* know."

"Did you know who her husband was having the affair with?" DeMarco asked.

"There were rumors it was with his ex-wife. Another rumor said it was with a nurse at the hospital."

A pretty accurate grapevine apparently runs through Amber Hills, Kate thought.

"Would you happen to have any other rumors you think might have a great deal of truth to them?" Kate asked. "Please understand, we're not looking for gossip. We're simply trying to get the entire story as we try to find the person responsible for these murders."

"Well, Lacy Thurmond was a sweetheart of a woman. I knew her pretty well but not enough to call her a friend. She was very involved in her church and was a good mother from what I understand. It's a shame her husband was such a miserable excuse for a man."

"Did you know him well?" Kate asked.

"No. Once I found out he was cheating on his wife, I didn't care to know anything at all about him."

"Well, how about Julie, your neighbor? We've spoken to some of her friends and they claim to know nothing the least bit negative about the Hicks family. Of course, it's hard to gauge the honesty of a group of friends. Would you say you could be an impartial party?"

"I suppose. Certainly a better source than those friends she kept. No woman should be *that* concerned about looking ten years younger than you actually are. Now, Julie and I would speak from time to time if we happened to be outdoors at the same time. She had me over for dinner once or twice last year after my husband passed away. But I wasn't close with her...not like those idiot friends of hers."

"Do you know if there was anyone in her life who was close to her that was *not* in her usual circle of friends?"

"Well, sure. I tell you, the sanctity of marriage means nothing to people anymore, now does it? Julie's husband was always on the road, traveling. No way to treat a marriage if you ask me. I started seeing this car in front of the Hicks house late at night about four months ago. I thought nothing of it until I saw a man get into it after coming out of the house early in the morning."

Kate dared to hope this would turn out to be a lead. But it was evident that Caroline Manners was a gossipy old lady with nothing better to do than to pry into the lives of others. She served as a great resource for information but there was no telling how much of that information might be accurate.

"You're certain of this?" Kate asked.

"Positive. I've been getting up with this weak bladder of mine at least three times a night for about two years now. Bladder infection from several years ago just never let them get back to their proper state. So I'm up at all hours. Sometimes when I get up for that four o'clock trip to the toilet, I just stay awake." She frowned and shook her head. "Sorry. That bordered on the entirely-too-personal, didn't it?"

"That's quite all right," Kate said. "But you say you actually saw this man leaving her home?"

"Yes. I saw him once but I saw the car three different times."

"Was it anyone you know?" DeMarco asked. "Anyone you've seen before?"

"No," Caroline said. "And I almost thought about taking down the number on the plates. But I didn't; I figured it's really none of my business."

Kate had to bite back a smile at that comment. "Do you recall the kind of car it was?" she asked.

"A newer one. Pretty sure it was a Honda. Gray or silver. Oh, and there *is* one more thing. Hell, I damn near forgot all about this little detail. When he was coming out, he had a jacket or hooded sweatshirt or something in his hand. He put it on as he was about halfway down the sidewalk. There was a logo and business name on the back of it. Pritchard Auto Glass."

"Did you get a good look at his face?" DeMarco asked.

"Just the side and just for a second," Caroline answered. "A clean-shaven man from what I could see. Looked a little young…early twenties, maybe?"

"And how long ago was it when you actually saw him leaving Julie's house?" Kate asked.

"I'm not sure. No more than a month ago."

"And what about some of the other friends in her group?" Kate asked. "Can you tell us anything else about them?"

"I'm afraid not. I know that Wendy Hudson has a father in prison and that Taylor Woodward has a drinking problem. She was pulled over for a DUI a few weeks ago…for the second time, the way I hear it."

Kate nodded and got to her feet. She had managed to pluck one promising bit of information out of the gossipy old lady. She was starting to get the feeling that the entire conversation might slip into pure gossip if they stayed much longer, though.

"Ms. Manners, we certainly appreciate your time," she said, already taking a step toward the door. DeMarco followed, also seemingly glad to be getting away from what looked to be devolving into a gossip-fest.

"Of course," Caroline said. The abrupt nature of her tone made it clear that she was disappointed her company was leaving so soon.

The agents made their exit as politely as they could. Caroline stood at the door and watched them get into the car, perhaps already twisting the story for entertaining her own circle of friends later.

"Sweet old lady," Kate said ironically.

"Or nosy old bitch," DeMarco countered.

"Either way, it looks like we got a lead," Kate said. What she didn't add was that it was, at most, a weak lead. She kept it quiet though because when a case was offering no clues or leads, even the smallest of breakthroughs could often serve as the motivation needed to get the case moving along.

With that hope pushing her, Kate got behind the wheel and headed out of Amber Hills while DeMarco pulled up the address for Pritchard Auto Glass.

CHAPTER TWENTY SIX

Broad Street was beginning to thicken up with afternoon rush hour traffic when Kate turned the car into the parking lot of Pritchard Auto Glass. The lot was mostly empty, indicating that this was the slower time of the day for the business. It was set up like an actual auto garage, with bay doors to let vehicles inside the garage where some of the work was done. There was also an open space to the side of the building where a few vehicles were parked, one of which was in the midst of getting its rear window replaced.

Kate and DeMarco walked inside and approached the front counter. One man was inputting a customer's information into a computer while another smiled widely at them. "Can I help you?" he asked.

Neither of these men were the young man Caroline Manners had mentioned; they were both easily forty or older.

"Yes," Kate said, getting so close to the counter that she was nearly pressed against it. She set her ID on the counter long enough for the man to see it and then pocketed it. "We're looking for a young man that likely works here. Maybe in his early twenties or so. We don't have a name or a clear description, so we were hoping to maybe walk around the place to see if anyone stands out to us."

"Well, the manager has already left, so I don't know if I can grant that sort of permission."

"If you need us to, one of us can call him," DeMarco said. "But I know it's getting close to quitting time and I really can't afford to wait much longer. But if you want to hang around after closing time…"

Well played, Kate thought, again finding herself impressed at the way DeMarco approached things.

"Fine, okay," the man said. "Besides the two of us, there are only two other guys here anyway, Roger and Billy. We've got Diane who is out on vacation and then Wyatt, the manager, who already left."

"Where would we find Roger and Billy?" DeMarco asked.

"Out in the side lot, putting a back glass in."

"Thanks," Kate said, the word leaving her lips as she turned toward the door.

She and DeMarco walked back out and headed for the repair lot on the side of the building. They approached slowly as Kate took a moment to study the two men who were currently replacing a window on a red Ford Explorer. One was an African-American man who looked to be no older than thirty. The other was a skinny-looking man who did indeed look rather young. He had just enough hair on his face to be called a five o'clock shadow.

Given that Caroline Manners had not expressly said that Julie Hicks's late night visitor had been African-American, Kate assumed that the skinny man was the one they were looking for. But she also knew that even *that* was a stretch. The sweatshirt Caroline Manners had seen the man put on could have been a promotional item or had once belonged to someone else—a brother or father, perhaps. There was no guarantee that the man with the sweatshirt leaving Julie's home had been an actual employee of Pritchard Auto Glass.

Kate gave DeMarco a little nod, giving her the go-ahead to kick things off. DeMarco stepped forward gladly. Kate noticed the way she slightly pushed the front of her open jacket to the side. This revealed her holstered sidearm, making it apparent that she was here with a law enforcement agency. It removed the need for her to pull out her ID, a tactic that was useful in not overly alarming people. Kate smiled, recognizing once again that DeMarco was damned good at what she did.

"Excuse me," DeMarco said. "I'm Agent DeMarco with the FBI and I need to speak with you for a moment, please."

Both men stared at her, looking equally confused.

"Which one?" the African-American asked.

"Whichever one of you knew Julie Hicks," DeMarco said.

Genius, Kate thought. The mention of Julie's name struck an immediate chord with the skinny man. And once it struck, he didn't even try to hide it. He looked scared and a little sad.

"I knew her," he said, raising his hand in an unsure manner. When he realized what he was doing, he lowered it. "What's going on?"

"Can we talk in private?" DeMarco asked.

"The break room, I guess," the man said. "Is…what is it? Did you guys find who killed her?"

"We can talk about all of that in a second," Kate said. "For now, why not just lead us to the break room."

The young man did exactly that. Kate could tell from the way he walked that he was trembling. It certainly wasn't a show of guilt but was more than enough to tell Kate that he was nervous—

whether about sleeping with a married woman or something deeper, though, was anyone's guess.

***

The break room was a small little corner in the back of the shop. There was a Keurig coffee machine and two empty boxes that had once held donuts. Other than that and a mini-fridge, Pritchard Auto Glass offered very little in the way of a break room. The young man had introduced himself as Billy Cosgrove as he took a seat at the break room table. He asked for their names and then asked to see ID.

Kate and DeMarco entertained him, showing their badges and IDs. There was one other chair at the break room table but neither of them took it. Kate leaned against the small counter while DeMarco stood her ground on the other side of the table.

"Rumor has it," DeMarco said, "that you were sleeping with Julie Hicks. Is that true?"

"Shit," Billy said. "Did her husband find out?"

"No," DeMarco said. "But her neighbor did. You're apparently not the best at keeping a good cover when you're out and about at night."

"So he doesn't know?"

"No," Kate said. "And there's no reason to tell him. But we were hoping you could maybe shed some light on Julie—that you could reveal some things about her that we might not have picked up from her husband or her friends."

"For starters, how did you two get involved?" DeMarco asked.

"Well, she brought her car in a few weeks back—maybe five or six weeks ago. The front window on the driver's side got busted by some kid throwing a baseball in their neighborhood. We fixed it and when she was here, she sort of seemed flirty with me. Nothing serious, and nothing I really even thought much of, you know? But she came back a few days later saying that the window wouldn't go down. So we checked it and found some fragments of glass from the first window in it. We had to order a new window and she seemed sort of pissed about it, saying she had a busy schedule and all. So we volunteered to come out to her house to do it. So they sent me out because it's a pretty easy job. Just me. She came out and talked to me a bit. When I knocked on her door to tell her the job was done, she invited me in. And I said yes. She was really flirty and dressed in this tight shirt and…"

He stopped here, realizing that he was speaking to two women. He blushed a bit, looked away from them, and then carried on.

"We started messing around. I saw pictures of her and her husband on the fridge in the kitchen. I asked her where he was and she said he was out of town—that he was always out of town because of his work. One thing led to another and we ended up having sex in her kitchen."

"So she was the aggressor?" Kate asked.

"Absolutely."

"And who initiated seeing one another again?"

"Her. But she made it clear to me that she wanted no relationship. She would not leave her husband. She just wanted something fun to do while he was away. She came out and told me she was just living out a wild side she'd never lived out in college."

"So this was an ongoing thing for how long?"

"About four or five weeks. The last time I saw her was two days before she died."

"Did you sleep with her then?"

"We had sex every time we saw one another. She was trying out all these things with me that she'd never done before. She was using me and, quite frankly, that was perfectly okay with me."

"So in this time with her, did she ever reveal anything about her personal life to you?" Kate asked. "Any people you heard of that might be upset with her?"

"No. Again…not trying to brag or be a smart ass, but there was never really any talking. I did ask her one time why she chose me and she said it was because I was different. She never explained it, but I knew what she meant."

"And what did she mean, exactly?" DeMarco asked.

"I was like hired help almost. Not someone from her neighborhood with its picket fences and expensive houses. She wanted a guy from the other side of town, you know? She wanted to feel like she was doing something *really* wrong."

"And you were okay with that?" Kate asked.

Billy looked at her with an incredulous expression on his face. "At the risk of sounding crude, yes. I was having regular sex— regular *rough* sex—with a hot older woman at least twice a week and there were no strings attached. Yes. I was okay with it."

"You never stopped to think about her husband and what it could do to their marriage?"

"No. I figure if he cared that much for her, he wouldn't stay on the road so much."

"Did she ever talk about any of her friends?"

He grinned nervously and nodded. "Yeah. Said she had a group of friends that all lived in the neighborhood. Most of them were stay-at-home moms or women that worked from home. Boring husbands with boring jobs. She told me she was going to arrange for a threesome with us and one of her friends but it never happened."

"What sort of people did she say her friends were?" Kate asked.

"She never went into detail about it but I got the gist that they were just like her. They slept around from time to time. Sort of adventurous, trying to live wild exciting lives before they got too old."

Kate knew she'd reached the end of the conversation. Billy was starting to sound like he was bragging and she was getting frustrated. She was all but certain he had no hand in the murders; there was no way he'd so openly admit to a sexual relationship with Julie Hicks if he was guilty.

"The night she was killed…where were you?" Kate asked.

"At home. Sleeping. Had a few too many beers with some friends and ended up passing out early."

"Any proof of this?" DeMarco asked.

"I think I have the receipt from the bar. I took a cab home, too. Paid with my debit card, so I can get that receipt if you need it."

Kate sighed and got to her feet. "Don't bother. Also, have you told anyone about your little excursions?"

"I told Roger, the guy I was working with when you got here. But I never told him a name."

"For the respect of the deceased and her family, please keep it quiet," Kate said.

"I absolutely will."

Kate and DeMarco left the break room, leaving a very shaken Billy Cosgrove behind them with a reflective yet sad look on his face.

"Now what?" DeMarco asked.

Kate wasn't accustomed to feeling defeated but she could feel it sinking into her bones, into her heart. She wasn't quite discouraged just yet but it was hard to stay upbeat.

"Now I want to go see my granddaughter again," Kate said. "And while I'm doing that, you think about what we'll have for dinner. It's going to be a long night of poring over case files, I'm afraid."

DeMarco nodded, although there was a disappointed look on her face. Apparently, this was not the high-octane experience she had been hoping to experience while partnered with the quasi-famous Agent Kate Wise.

And Kate understood it perfectly. So far, it wasn't panning out the way she had expected, either.

CHAPTER TWENTY SEVEN

He'd been planning this one for a very long time. In a way, the first two had been practice. This was the one he had always had in mind when he'd started. And those first two women had proven to him that he had no real problem with killing. It seemed natural and almost therapeutic. It made him envy the jobs that men back in the Middle Ages had enjoyed—jobs like executioner or the general in charge of whatever group oversaw the torture and dismemberment of their enemies.

This woman was different. He knew her much better than he had known the others. He'd seen her naked, had watched her strip in front of a mirror in appreciation of herself—or, perhaps, in fear that her thirty-something body would maybe not be perfect much longer.

This time, he felt a sense of urgency. He'd allowed himself to enjoy the planning and anticipation of the other two. But now he knew the cops were on to him. They were crawling around Amber Hills like ants, looking for whatever honey had been spilled. Of course, when he had started it all, he knew the authorities would eventually become a problem. And while he certainly didn't want to go to prison, it was an outcome that he was ready for.

He'd been very quick and efficient with the first two. He'd planned it all out but had not overthought it. Each act had taken no more than five seconds. But this next one…he thought he might stretch it out.

One thing was different this time, though. Something that made it perhaps a bit riskier, but he knew her schedule, knew it had to be different. He had to strike during the day. And with all of the fucking cop cars around the neighborhood, it might be tricky.

So he chose to blend in. He drove into the neighborhood like he belonged there. He even gave a little cursory wave to the cop who was stationed at the entrance. The cop nodded to him, bored and featureless.

He drove down the main stretch of Amber Hills, a wider road called Amber Drive. He took a left and within seconds was passing the Thurmond residence. There were no police cars there anymore but he still made every attempt not to look in the direction of the house. He passed by it like a motorist trying to avoid looking at a particularly bad car accident.

Then he saw the house. He saw the perfectly manicured landscaping and the lush green yard. He saw the porch swing, the large plants bordering the front door. And, keeping with his appearance of normalcy, he went so far as to even pull into the driveway, right behind the car that was already parked there.

Her car.

He took a moment to collect his thoughts, to collect his nerve. The dashboard clock read 6:15. He knew her schedule well. She would have just come back home from the gym about twenty minutes ago. She was either in the shower or lying on the back deck to catch some sun. But seeing how the day was overcast, he was thinking she'd be in the shower.

Upstairs. In the bedroom. By herself.

He smiled. As he walked to the porch, he wasn't sure what he was the most excited about: catching her naked in the shower or plunging the knife between her breasts.

***

Taylor Woodward knew she was attractive. She was thirty-one and could still catch the eyes of the younger men in the gym. But the thing of it was that she had worked her ass off to stay so hot. She dieted, she ate right, and she exercised regularly. Her mother had let herself go around the age of forty and when she'd died two years ago, she'd been almost three hundred pounds. Seeing her mother's chubby face in that open casket had driven Taylor to continue her healthy lifestyle. And although she knew she often carried it too far, she didn't care. She liked having her abs, her perfectly toned ass, her still-perky breasts.

And more than that, she liked the looks she got at the gym and the pool. And she loved the way her husband sometimes looked at her—in the same way boys had looked at her when she was a teenager, a way that made her think she was all he was thinking about.

As she came to the end of her shower, she wished her husband was there with her. Unlike most of her friends, she had never had an affair. She knew she had all the options in the world if she decided to have one—from the eighteen-year-olds at the gym to the wealthy forty- and fifty-year-olds in the neighborhood.

But she loved her husband. And as the water cascaded off of her body, she wished he was there, under the water with her. Sex had gotten a little formulaic as of late. She couldn't remember the last time he'd taken her by surprise, out of nowhere, a little rough and—

She smiled when she heard the bathroom door open behind her. She knew it was a little after six and that his work often brought him home as early as seven or as late as nine. But sometimes, every now and then, he'd manage to come home early. And if he was coming into the bathroom knowing she was in there, maybe he had the same thing on his mind—a little afternoon delight in the shower.

"I'm almost done," she said flirtatiously. "But I can take another one if I happen to get dirty again."

He said nothing but she could see him moving through the fog and haze of the steam and the misted over glass of the shower door. She smiled; it was good to see just how eager he still made her.

She turned to face the back of the shower, as that's where he'd come in. The door opened but he did not come inside. Instead, it was just an arm. It grabbed her by the shoulder and pulled her forward. She lost her footing on the wet shower floor. As she fell, he caught her by the hair and pulled her out of the open door.

Electric pain raced around her skull as she was pulled by the hair. She screamed, not fully sure what the hell was happening. But then she was thrown to the floor and he was on her.

She saw the face then and realized who it was.

You...

She opened her mouth to scream again and this time a clubbing right hand came sailing at her mouth. She felt a tooth come out as her mouth filled with blood. She was afraid she'd choke on it but then that fear was replaced by an intense pain, a pain so blinding it was unreal.

It was then that she realized she could not breathe, that something had happened to her chest.

And then she saw the knife as he pulled it out of her.

She saw it one more time as it came sailing down toward her and although she felt it enter her again, she barely registered it.

She looked upward, to the ceiling, to the gathering steam of the shower, and prayed for it to end quickly as the shape of the man above her blurred into blackness until there was nothing left.

CHAPTER TWENTY EIGHT

Kate could not get over how the simple act of holding her newborn granddaughter was able to recharge her, but it did. It was both a mental and physical jolt to the system. And while it didn't have quite the same powerful effect as holding Melissa for the first time when she had been born, it was very similar. She assumed it had something to do with the instinctual human need to carry on a bloodline, to revel in the fact that she was holding a third generation in her hands.

She was marveling over this as she sat with DeMarco in her dining room over dinner. DeMarco had chosen Chinese for their dinner, which was absolutely fine with Kate. She usually tried to eat healthy but given the way the last two days had gone, she figured she could allow herself a cheat meal.

"You know something I'd like to find out from the police?" DeMarco said as she studied a file and swirled a lo mein noodle onto her fork. "I'd like to know what the police at the Amber Hills gates are looking for. There are no neighborhood decals or stickers of any kind on the cars for that neighborhood."

"That's a good point," Kate said. "And from what I can see, they aren't stopping people that come in or go out."

"And really, none of that would make a difference if the killer is actually an Amber Hills resident," DeMarco pointed out.

Kate nodded. These were all good points, ones that she had considered before. But until they found something relevant and tangible to go on, they could only guess. In her own head, she had started to compile a list of pros and cons. It was a list that might be made by a killer that would use Amber Hills as a killing field of sorts. For a killer to choose such a place to strike two times in a small window of time seemed both risky and, quite frankly, genius.

The biggest pro, of course, was that the victims were easy pickings. And based on the women he had selected—very attractive women who tended to stay at home, in their late twenties or early thirties—Amber Hills provided a promising group of victims. By staying in one centralized location, it was easier to pick your targets and to get a proper lay of the land. If the killer lived elsewhere in town, it also kept the investigation centralized in one place while he was very likely hiding somewhere else.

But then there were the cons. In a small area, the likelihood of someone seeing him would be much greater. It also meant that escaping through smaller side streets within the neighborhood would make a fast getaway virtually impossible. Someone would notice a speeding car and, in such a neighborhood, would likely report it out of fear of kids getting hurt.

If we had even just a hint *of motive, it would help wonders,* Kate thought as she closed one of the several files she had accumulated.

Her phone rang as she reached for another file. The name and number were familiar and for a moment, she almost didn't answer it. But she figured maybe stepping away and shifting her mind to something else for even just a few moments could be a massive help.

Reading Allen Goldman's name, she grabbed up her phone and stepped away from the table. "This will just take a moment," she told DeMarco as she hurried into the living room.

"Hey, Allen," she said, taking the call.

"Hey," he said. "I was honestly expecting to have to leave a message."

"Then why not just text?"

"I was hoping for the off chance you would actually answer. Also, the other night on the porch you told me to call next time. So here I am…calling."

"I appreciate that," she said. "What can I do for you?"

"For one, wrap up this case you're on by Friday. I want to take you out to dinner."

"Well, I've got more than this case right now," she said. "Melissa had her baby."

"What? She wasn't due for like another what…five or six weeks?"

"Yeah. Little Michelle came early. She and Melissa are doing fine, though. I've already been able to hold her twice."

"That's great, Kate. So you're officially a grandmother now. How's it feel?"

"Better than I thought. It's sort of amazing, actually."

"Good. Well, for you, anyway. Sounds like your life is absolutely nuts right now. My timing…it's just wretched, huh?"

"It is. But that's okay. We can—"

She was interrupted by a beep on her phone—an incoming call. She quickly checked the display and saw that it was Chief Budd calling.

123

"Speaking of bad timing," she said, "I have to get this. It's about the case."

"Okay," he said, trying to hide the sigh in his voice but failing.

"But Allen...thanks for calling. And maybe do it again soon, okay?"

"Absolutely. G'night, Kate. "

Kate switched over to the incoming call, hoping Budd calling meant that there was finally some sort of break. Maybe from the coroner or someone on his investigative team.

"This is Wise," she answered.

"Agent Wise, this is Randall Budd. Are you still in Richmond or have you gone back to DC?"

"Still in Richmond. Why? What's up?"

"We've got another body. This one is very fresh."

"Amber Hills?" Kate asked.

"Yes."

"What's the address? We can be there in twenty minutes."

Budd gave her the address and she was not at all surprised to find that it was on the same street Lacy Thurmond had lived on. She ended the call and headed into the kitchen where DeMarco was eating an egg roll and looking through the coroner's reports.

"Study session is over," Kate said. "Budd just called. There's been another murder."

"Holy shit," DeMarco said. "How long ago?"

"He says it's fresh. No details yet. Let's just get over there as soon as we can."

Yet even before the comment was out of Kate's mouth, DeMarco was shoveling the remainder of the egg roll into her mouth and getting up from the table. Kate was starting to appreciate DeMarco more and more. Her go-get-'em attitude and teachability made her miss Logan a little less. Though, to be honest, she did miss the sarcastic back and forth they had shared most of the time.

But maybe such a thing took time to develop between partners. While she had not quite reached that point with her first partner, it had come naturally for her and Logan. And now, with DeMarco as her partner, she was beginning to understand that all partnerships evolved in their own different way. And as she and DeMarco raced out of her house, she looked forward to seeing where this new partnership would go.

Hopefully, she thought, *it will lead to closing this case.*

As she got into the car and slammed it into Drive, she thought of that first partner from twenty-seven years ago. She'd partnered with him for nearly ten years and they had never gotten close emotionally. But he had been one hell of a mentor and during her time away from the bureau, she'd thought of him often.

And he was there again, at the edge of her mind, as she sped toward Amber Hills. She wondered what his take on this case would be. His wisdom and experience may see the case from a different perspective. She mulled over this, wondering if he'd even take her calls anymore.

It was something to consider. If this next crime scene offered nothing of substance, maybe she'd reach out

But she couldn't go there yet. Instead, she chose to hope that the next crime scene would offer something—perhaps some clue, no matter how small or seemingly insignificant.

Besides, even at fifty-five years of age, her life was still evolving. She was a grandmother now. She had a man who was very interested in her. And she was back on the job, on a case that was proving to be among her toughest. To dredge the past back up seemed to make no sense.

So with the present and the future in mind, they closed in on Amber Hills as night slowly started to fall around Richmond.

CHAPTER TWENTY NINE

The house was just like any of the others along most stretches of Amber Hills. The only thing that made it stand out was the blue and red flashing lights from the police sirens, strobing against the dusk. When Kate pulled her car in behind one of the six police cars on the scene, she noticed that there were other police cars parked all along the sides of the streets. It seemed that the police were doing everything they could to keep prying eyes from getting a good glimpse at what was going on.

As she walked up the sidewalk, she saw Chief Budd on the porch, speaking to a pair of officers. Kate hurried toward him and when he noticed her approaching, he instantly stopped the conversation with the other officers.

"That was quick," Budd said.

"You said this one was fresh. I wanted to keep it like that. Where's the body?"

"Come with me," he said. "I've already told everyone that when you got here, it's your show. CSI is even going to wait until you're done. Unless you want them."

"Just keep them close," Kate said. "I'm not trying to slow this down for anyone."

"Well, that shouldn't be a problem. So far, it seems as cut and dried as all the rest. Only...well, I guess dried is the wrong word."

"What?" DeMarco asked, confused.

"You'll see," Budd said as he led them inside.

He led them down the main hall to where a flight of stairs led to the second floor. He marched down the upstairs hallway, into the master bedroom. Kate saw that the bathroom door was open and as they neared it, she could actually smell the blood.

As she headed for the door, an agonizing wail filled the house. It was a male's voice, coming from downstairs.

"That's the husband," Budd said. "He came home and found his wife exactly like you're about to see her. He called nine-one-one and the first officer on the scene found him passed out in his own puke right over there," he said, pointing to the far side of the king-sized bed.

Kate carefully stepped into the bathroom. It was muggy and moist, but that was not nearly the worst of it. A woman lay on the bathroom floor, staring up at the ceiling. She was completely naked, making the stab wounds to her chest, abdomen, and pelvic area easy to see.

While the stab wounds were grisly indeed, it was the woman's face that shook Kate. She knew this woman. She had seen her in the last few days.

Behind her, DeMarco gave voice to what was on Kate's lips. "That's Taylor Woodward."

"You know her?" Budd asked.

"Not personally," Kate said. "We questioned her with another woman yesterday. They were both friends of Julie Hicks and Lacy Thurmond. The other woman present was Wendy Hudson. And please send a car to her house right now. Three out of four friends is *not* a coincidence. Wendy Hudson needs to be placed in protective custody as far as I'm concerned."

"I'll get on that right now," Budd said. When he quickly turned away from the bathroom door, he seemed glad to do so.

DeMarco stepped up beside Kate, both women now standing in the bathroom. There was a pool of standing water at the back of the shower, puddled up on the floor. Some of the copious amounts of blood that had spilled from Taylor's body had mingled with it, turning it into an almost pretty kind of fractal pattern.

"This isn't exactly the same as the others," Kate said.

"I noticed that, too," DeMarco said. "There's a stab wound just above the vagina. More than a stab; he stabbed and then sliced up and down. It's intentional. If you're aiming for the heart and the stomach, you don't miss by *that* much."

"And that's a pretty blatant spot to aim for," Kate said, doing her best not to grimace at the sight. "Like you said…this was intentional. It's the first sign from this killer that this was more than just murder. I think this might be the first sign of a murder of emotion. Sexual in nature, I'd safely assume."

"So why her and not the others?" DeMarco asked.

"I guess we need to find that out."

The tortured wailing of the husband filled the house again. There was rage in his screams as well as sorrow. He wanted vengeance. The lacing of obscenities that followed his mournful cries was further proof of this.

Kate stepped further into the bathroom, careful to watch for any other stray water. She hunkered down and looked for any stray streaks or marks on the white tiled floor. While she saw nothing of the sort, she did see a small white fragment of something, all the way over by the edge of the shower.

She inched a little closer, careful not to disturb the body. With a few more steps, she realized what she was looking at. It was a portion of a tooth.

"She was hit," Kate said. "See this piece of tooth?"

DeMarco nodded and then got closer to the body. She leaned down and looked at Taylor Woodward's face. "Very slight bruising just above her upper lip on the left side. If she was struck, it'll be more than enough to get a print."

"This guy's smart," she said. "Not a single print yet—not on a body, on a doorknob, nothing. I'm suspecting he wears gloves."

"Any theories on how this played out?" DeMarco asked.

"All the water on the floor makes me think he just grabbed her right out of the shower," Kate said. "But the lack of any real sign of a struggle makes me think it was another case of Taylor knowing the killer, or at least expecting someone she knew. He got in easily enough. I'd even venture that he knew she was showering."

"You think this is another affair-related thing, too? That sort of knowledge about someone's schedule…"

"Well, but the husband had to have come home very soon after she was killed. If the killer was a lover or something, you'd think they'd be more careful with their time tables." She looked around the bathroom one more time and shook her head. "Something just doesn't add up here."

"We need to speak with the husband," DeMarco said.

"For sure. But from the sound of it, he's not in the best state. In the meantime, I think we should have a look around the rest of the house. Maybe even outside."

They both slowly left the bathroom, Kate giving the body one last look. As grisly as it seemed, her eyes kept going back to that stab wound below the waist. It showed intention, maybe even the kind of malice and spite that had been absent from the other two scenes.

He's either starting to enjoy the act of killing more or there was something different about Taylor Woodward, Kate thought. *If it's the latter, that could point to motive or a solid lead.*

She also thought about something Tate O'Brien had said when she'd spoken with him.

DeMarco had asked him: *"So you did it for love?"*

His response had been: *No. It was just my wife for love. It was out of rage for her lover. And that third one…if I'm being honest, I just got carried away. It was almost…fun by that point."*

She wondered if this killer was going through a similar evolution.

They headed back downstairs to the sounds of an anguished husband. She'd heard similar cries at murder scenes before but it was something she had never gotten used to. Even when she and DeMarco circled the property for any signs of breaking and entering, the husband's wails followed her, sending little chills into her heart.

CHAPTER THIRTY

Some of Budd's men managed to talk the husband down from his heartbroken state. At some point, his mother had showed up to console him. Kate assumed the mother had done more good than the policemen. Kate and DeMarco were back in the bedroom, looking around for any signs that the killer might have been looking for something in particular, when Budd came for them.

"He's still obviously in a wrecked state, but he wants to speak with you. He understands that the sooner he does, the better chance we have of finding the killer. He's currently across the street with his neighbors. His mother had to drag him out of this house kicking and screaming."

On the way back downstairs, Budd filled them in on what he had picked up on while around the husband. His name was Daryl Woodward. He worked as an insurance salesman in town. His office was less than twenty minutes away from home but it sometimes took him as much as forty-five minutes to get home from work if he got caught in traffic at the wrong time. When his mother had gotten there, she'd taken him out of the house, not wanting him to grieve knowing that his dead wife was in the bathroom over his head.

Kate and DeMarco walked across the street to the neighbor's house. A few cops were on the porch, speaking with the neighbors. They acknowledged the agents as they passed but said nothing. The entire porch and house beyond was veiled in an overwhelming silence.

When they entered the living room, they found Daryl Woodward and his mother sitting on the couch. They were huddled together in a sad embrace. Kate hated to break their silence but she took a moment to introduced DeMarco and herself. She noted how Daryl Woodward nodded and followed her with his eyes like he was in some sort of dreaming state. The mother, who introduced herself as Miranda Thomas, held her son close as if he were a fragile kid who had scraped his knee on the playground. There was nothing creepy or overprotective about it as far as Kate was concerned. She was simply a mother, heartbroken for her suddenly distraught son.

"Mr. Woodward, I can't imagine how you must be feeling right now," Kate said. "So I'm going to only ask basic questions to make this as quick as possible."

He nodded his understanding, His bottom lip was trembling and his eyes were both wide and tired-looking at the same time. It was a rather creepy-looking expression.

"Do you know what Taylor had been doing before you arrived home?" Kate asked.

"Yeah. She had just gotten back from the gym. Her gym bag was at the foot of the bed. I don't think she'd even cleaned it out yet."

"How often does she go to the gym?"

"Three or four times a week. She prefers to go later in the afternoon because the crowd isn't as bad."

"How was she holding up as of late with the deaths of her two friends, Julie Hicks and Lacy Thurmond?"

"It hurt her. She cried hardest for Julie. They were pretty close, I think."

"Mr. Woodward, I know it's a hard question, but can you think of anyone who might have wanted to do this to Taylor?"

He shook his head and started wailing instantly. It was a deep groaning that came out of him in something akin to a grunt. Kate watched him valiantly try to fight it off so he could answer their questions. It was the first time in a while that Kate felt like a terrible person. She was interrupting his grieving, stopping him from properly mourning his wife. But, as Budd had said, certainly Daryl knew that the sooner he spoke, the better the chance of finding the killer.

"Mr. Woodward, I have to ask you some very hard questions now. Questions you're going to hate me for asking. And you may not want your mother here."

"It's okay," Daryl said. "I'm expecting them. After what happened with Julie and Lacy...I know what you're going to ask. And no. I can guarantee you that she was not having an affair."

"But you acknowledge that her friends were?" DeMarco asked.

"Julie was. She told Taylor all about it. But if Lacy was having an affair, it was being kept very quiet. Pretty sure her husband was messing around behind Lacy's back though."

Miranda Thomas seemed appalled at all of this information but said nothing.

"What about social situations?" Kate asked. "Was there anything you know of that Julie, Lacy, and Taylor were all involved in?"

"No. I mean, nothing like clubs or anything like that. We all have memberships at the same pool, but that's about it. It was just the women, mind you. There were never dates with all of us as couples. Hell, I've never even met Julie's husband."

"You told Chief Budd that you work close to your home," DeMarco said. "What time do you usually get home?"

"Some nights it's as early as seven. But there are nights when it's as late as eight o'clock. I try to sneak home as early as five on the days where I've busted my ass but the damned traffic makes it hard, you know?"

He was sobbing as he spoke, making some of the words very difficult to understand. Kate couldn't help but wonder if, as he spoke, he was beginning to understand that for the next few years, it might not matter much *when* he got home from work.

"One last question," Kate said. "When you were on your way in—that is, once you made it into Amber Hills coming from work—did you pass any cars that you noticed were speeding or maybe even driving recklessly?"

"No, I didn't notice anything like that," he said.

Kate knew that Daryl Woodward was doing his absolute best. But she also knew that he'd be much more effective in terms of useful information in the coming days. Given that, she took out one of her old business cards, another of the relics she had held onto in the year between retirement and being brought back in to the bureau several days ago. She nearly handed it to him but then realized that the number on it was to the old bureau phone she'd had back then.

Got to get news ones, she thought, a little embarrassed. In the context of what Daryl Woodward was going through, though, it felt stupid.

"Mr. Woodward, would you mind giving me your phone number? I'm going to text you my number. And in the coming days, I want you to call me if you think of anything else. I'm very interested in anything Taylor and her friends might have been involved in together. Or maybe the names of people you heard Taylor talking about that only came up on occasion. That sort of thing. Can you do that?"

"Sure," he said. "I wish I could help. I wish there was something…"

An explosion of grief came out of him in that moment. Daryl sank into his mother's shoulder and cried. He screamed so hard that Kate feared he might pass out. He had, after all, vomited from the sight of his wife less than an hour and a half ago. She couldn't imagine the trauma he was going through.

Only, she *could*. She remembered what it had been like seeing Michael after he'd been shot. She remembered that empty feeling, the sensation of being detached from the world.

Miranda looked at them with her own tears in her eyes. "Please...go," she said. "I don't mean that in a disrespectful way, but you can clearly see that he's in no shape..."

"Of course," Kate said. She'd wanted to exchange numbers with him, but she could manage that some other way. "Thank you for your time," she added as she stepped away.

DeMarco followed along, clearly not on the same page. Still, the younger agent said nothing until they were back outside, headed across the street back to the Woodward residence.

"That's it?" she asked. "That's all the questions we had for him?"

"For now," she said. "He needs to clear his head. I can't push him to answer questions that his grief is going to manipulate or make foggy."

"He did seem sincere, huh?" DeMarco asked.

"He did. But there's something else in his moaning and crying. There's rage there, I think. If he thinks of something, he'll call."

"Poor guy," DeMarco said. "You think I even need to look into him? Maybe I should call some of his co-workers to make sure he was there this afternoon?"

"Can't hurt," Kate said. But really, that would just be checking off a box. Based on what she had seen, there was no way in hell Daryl Woodward was a suspect.

While DeMarco did some digging, trying to get the phone numbers of Daryl's co-workers, Kate went back into the house and looked for Budd. He was standing in the kitchen, comparing notes with a few other officers.

"He's still in no shape to talk right now," Kate told Budd. "He did his best but we're going to step away for a bit. When he's stable, I'd like for you to give him my number if you don't mind."

"I can do that," he said. He turned his back to the officer he had been speaking to and looked Kate in her eyes. When he spoke, his voice was much quieter than it had been three seconds ago. "Did you see *anything* that might help?" he asked, looking up toward the ceiling.

"A few things of note, but we don't know for sure yet," she said. "I'll keep you posted. I want to keep you and your force on this alongside us. The more, the merrier—and the better chance to wrap this damn thing up."

Budd sighed and rubbed at his temples. "I appreciate that. And I'll make sure Daryl Woodward gets your number."

Kate left, noting the defeated look on Budd's face. He was angry, sure, but he also looked beaten. It was the look of a man who had no idea what to do.

Honestly, she felt for him. She knew that they were doing their very best. There were policemen at every single Amber Hills entrance and, as of about ten minutes ago, there were two police cars parked in front of Wendy Hudson's home. She figured the next step would be to canvas the neighborhood, to send police officers door to door looking for even the most minuscule bit of information.

But she knew that such measures were usually kept as last resorts—a desperate grasp for *something.*

And if that's where they currently were on this case, there might be nothing more than disappointment ahead.

CHAPTER THIRTY ONE

Even after spending another half an hour at the crime scene and looking around the body, Kate and DeMarco were unable to find anything that was instantly beneficial. Kate, however, was more convinced than ever that Taylor Woodward would be the key to finding the killer. The focus on the genitals spoke volumes. Upon first glance, Kate had been pretty sure there had been no sexual activity involved in the murder, but of course, the coroner would have to be the one to confirm that.

There was also the punch to the face to be considered. It was not the killer's style based on what they'd seen at the other two scenes. Something about Taylor Woodward had apparently bothered him much more than Julie Hicks or Lacy Thurmond.

Due to the late hour, the door-to-door approach was nixed fairly quickly, though a few officers were sent out to neighboring houses of people who had known the Hicks, Thurmonds, and Woodwards relatively well. While Budd sent a few men out to tackle that assignment, Demarco had managed to find one of Daryl Woodward's co-workers who was able to meet with them on short notice.

Kate was driving to the address of the co-worker when her phone rang. There were so many loose ends on this case that she honestly had no idea who to expect on the other end. The voice she heard was, admittedly, not one she had expected to hear. It was Assistant Director Duran.

"Agent Wise, what is your current location?" he asked.

"There's been another murder," she said, feeling rather guilty for not notifying him sooner. "DeMarco and I are on the way to visit with a co-worker of the husband to make sure his story checks out."

"I know there's been another murder," he said. "When I gave you authority to work the case, I asked Chief Budd to keep me posted on any new developments. The victim is Taylor Woodward, right? Thirty-one years old, killed by multiple stab wounds to the chest and abdomen."

"That's right."

"Look, Wise...I won't lie about this: some of the other directors are thinking we made a mistake. There's grumbling about

135

jumping the gun on this, on letting you take this case. So as your acting director, I'm officially pulling you."

"Are you serious?"

"Yes. While we certainly don't blame you, this third victim makes this case much more of a priority. We'd like to task another agent to it. Maybe a few more. And before you argue, you need to think it through. As of right now, plans are still in place to have you come in and assist with cold cases. But if you remain on this and results aren't found quickly, I'm afraid a decision will be made to scrap that effort as well."

"You gave me three days," she said. "Less than three days, actually. And in those three days, my daughter went into labor five weeks early and I became a grandmother. I've been a little rushed."

"You're only proving my point further," Duran said. "You have a life outside of the bureau now. You should live it."

This is *my life,* she nearly said. But even the thought alone sounded sad and pathetic.

"So what was the point of all of this? Do you think I can't wrap this case?"

"I didn't say that. But the decision has been made. I'm sorry, Kate."

She didn't want to grovel (not that she ever would) and she didn't want to seem desperate or needy in front of DeMarco. So she was essentially stuck.

"Is the cold case option still open if I let this go?"

"I'm fairly certain of it. And like I said…there has been no official decision to pull you from those above me. But it's coming. If I can report to them that I've already done it, it makes things much smoother for the cold case option."

"Fine. Do it, then," she said.

It was an odd feeling. She was angry to have been given the opportunity only to have it yanked away from her a few days later. But at the same time, she was grateful; she knew that it was extremely rare for retired agents to get such an opportunity.

"I appreciate your understanding, Wise," Duran said. "DeMarco will remain on the case. I'll have assistance out there to accompany her by eight o'clock tomorrow morning."

"I'll let her know," Kate said. And while it may have been a bit unprofessional, Kate ended the call without a proper goodbye.

"That didn't sound good," DeMarco said.

"It wasn't. Because of the lack of results and a third victim, I've been pulled from the case."

"What the hell?"

Kate shrugged. "It makes sense. They were already taking a risk by letting me on it. The case got out of my hands and they can't afford the bad PR. It also potentially salvages one other opportunity for me. You're still on, though. He's sending people to assist you tomorrow."

"Still...this sucks."

Kate shrugged. "It does. But it is what it is."

"I'll keep you informed if you want me to."

Kate considered it for a moment and then shook her head. "Best not to. I need to remove myself from it completely. But I'm going to put in an excellent word for you. And who knows...maybe you and I can work together again in the future."

DeMarco said nothing. She just looked out the window and watched the night pass by.

"I'm going to take you back to the motel," Kate said. "You should still go meet with Daryl Woodward's co-worker."

"Sounds good," DeMarco said.

But DeMarco now looked just as defeated as Chief Budd had while standing in the Woodwards' kitchen. Kate tried to think of something to say, something inspiring and motivating, but nothing came to mind.

They continued the drive back to the motel in silence as a sense of failure filled the car like the stench of a dead animal on the side of the road.

***

For the second time that day, Kate found herself thinking about the first partner she'd had while working as an agent. His name was Jimmy Parker and he'd quickly become something of a mentor to Kate. She'd worked with him for eight years before he had been promoted to the position of assistant director of a field office in Atlanta. He'd eventually come back to DC to fill in for another director who had lost his job very suddenly. Jimmy had filled out the rest of his years in that position and retired a few years later. Kate had been thirty-eight when he'd retired.

She thought back to those years, startled to find that nearly twenty years had passed since she'd been thirty-eight. She knew that Jimmy was still alive and well, having gotten a brief phone call the week she'd retired last year. Jimmy was nearing eighty years of age and although he'd said nothing about it during that phone call one year ago, there had been a rumor circulating that he was fighting some form of cancer and wasn't looking too well.

When Kate returned home from dropping DeMarco off at the motel, her thoughts instantly went to Jimmy Parker. Perhaps it was her ability to finally sympathize with him—the retired mentor who had always made a point to call the bureau heads at least once a month to check on things—not because he felt he could really contribute any further but because he had simply never learned to let go of that life.

With no one to talk to and well aware of the dangers of internalizing things like failure and confusion when it came to bureau work, Kate found herself pulling up Jimmy's number on her cell phone. She stared at it for a moment, unsure. Would he appreciate this call or feel almost obligated to her?

Before she could overthink it, Kate pressed CALL. When the phone started ringing, she realized that it was closing in on ten o'clock at night. Was that too late to call a man who was slowly creeping up on eighty years of age?

Apparently not. He answered on the second ring and when he did, it was in a bright and cheerful voice.

"Kate Wise," he said as if he were announcing her presence to a large room. "How in the hell are you?"

"Still here," she said, not wanting to dump her issues on him right away.

"Is retirement suiting you?"

"No. it never really did. Maybe that's why I somehow ended up working another case this week."

"On official grounds?" Jimmy asked.

"More or less. It was short-lived, though."

"You'll have to teach me how you talked your way into that," Jimmy said. "I pestered them for years about maybe coming back on for part-time work."

"I doubt they saw it as pestering," Kate said. "How are you, Jimmy? A real answer, if you please."

"I'm getting old," he said with a creaky laugh. "Seventy-eight is a bitch. I have arthritis in my right hand. I had a knee replacement last year. My bladder is weaker than thin toilet paper and I'm having to go to the doctor at least once a month to keep a check on my heart and prostate."

"How are you spending your days?" she asked, realizing just how thin of a question it was the moment it was out of her mouth.

"Sitting around. I watch TV. I read. I'm part of a chess club but I'm the oldest member and these young kids are beating me pretty bad. So if you have tales of somehow getting back into work after retirement, I'd love to hear them."

"It's really not very exciting," Kate said.

Nevertheless, she found herself telling him the series of events that had occupied the last week or so of her life. From Debbie Meade asking her to look into the death of her daughter all the way up to Duran relieving her of her temporary bureau duties. She even went into scant details of the case, noting the way Jimmy gave a series of *wow*s and *you don't say*s in all the right places.

When she came to the end of it, she realized that she really *had* been privileged to get the opportunity. She just hoped her inability to wrap the case would not reflect poorly on DeMarco.

"So, this case," Jimmy said. "You believe this last victim stands out among the other two because of some of the details of the killing, yes?"

"Seems that way," Kate said.

"So that would suggest that the killer perhaps had some sort of grudge against her. And that would lead me to believe that there was some sort of personal beef between the two—either directly or indirectly."

"That's the assumption I'm running with, yes. But it doesn't matter. I'm not on the case anymore. And the agent who has it is highly competent. She's going to be amazing in a few years."

"You can let a case go just like that?"

"I have to," she said. "I became a grandmother the other night. I'm toying with the idea of dating again. My life is sort of evolving all around me. And maybe going back to work in such a capacity was a step back. Maybe I need to let go of the past."

"That's the worst-smelling bullshit I've ever heard," Jimmy said.

"The grumpy old man persona really fits you," Kate said.

"Oh, I know. And I wear it with pride. It lets me call out people when they're talking foolishness. Like you are. Take it from me: if you have the chance to get one or two more cases in—even if it's working mundane tasks on cold cases—take it. If not, you'll always wonder if you wasted one last shot."

She let this sink in, knowing that even the possibility of staying in the game on those cold case files would be a great opportunity. It was either that or resigning herself to the fact that the retired life was all she had waiting. And while there was a new granddaughter in the picture, she knew she also had to live her own life. Fifty-five, after all, was not the end of the world.

"So tell me about this granddaughter," Jimmy said.

And just like that, the man she had learned most of the bureau basics from had turned her away from painful self-reflection and toward joy. *Some things never change,* she thought as she told him all about Michelle, Melissa, and her growing family.

It was good to talk about those things...refreshing in a way. It made her wonder what it might be like to give Allen Goldman a chance. Even if there wasn't perfect chemistry between them, she'd at least have someone who was interested in her, who would be there to listen to her brag about her beautiful baby granddaughter and the things she hoped to do with her life now that she was retired.

She stayed on the phone for another half an hour with Jimmy Parker. It was good to reconnect with someone who had played such a pivotal role early in her career. It made her think of DeMarco again and how these last few days would not harm her future in any way.

She got off the phone with Jimmy feeling lighter, not so bogged down with the knowledge that Duran had benched her. She found peace in it and was able to refocus her mind on her future. She thought of Melissa and the baby, of maybe giving Allen a call tomorrow and taking him up on dinner on Friday.

Still, when she closed her eyes in search of sleep, there was something sinister at the core of all of those things. She could not help but see the floor of the master bathroom in the Woodwards' house and all of that blood mingling with the water, as if the world itself was trying to wash any evidence away.

CHAPTER THIRTY TWO

Kate woke up to the ringing of her cell phone. She had not set an alarm, deciding to let herself sleep as late as she could. But when she grabbed at the phone, she saw that the blue digital letters on her alarm clock read 8:05.

Eight hours of sleep, she thought to herself. *When was the last time that happened?*

She saw DeMarco's name on the display and got excited. Maybe something big had occurred last night, some big break in the case perhaps. Despite the calming talk with Jimmy last night, her heart could not help but leap at the prospect of some exciting news involving the events that had been taking place in Amber Hills.

"Hey, DeMarco," she answered. "Miss me already?"

"The way this morning is going, yeah...I miss you tons. Duran called me at seven to let me know that two agents are on their way down to work this with me. One is straight out of the academy."

"You'll manage it," Kate said. "Something has to turn up eventually."

"Well, we do have a few updates. First of all, the medical exam came back early this morning. There were absolutely no signs of sexual intercourse. So I guess the cut to the genitals was symbolic."

"Or just the killer having some morbid fun," Kate pointed out.

"We also picked up what looks to be a print. It was right along the edge of the shower door. But it was so wet, we don't think it's going to amount to much. Some hair was also pulled from the drain but we're expecting it all to belong to the Woodwards."

"Thanks for the updates," Kate said. "But you don't have to do that. I'm off of it. You don't owe me updates."

"I know. But I know it has to piss you off to be put on something like this after a year away only to be pulled off of it. It's honestly not fair to you. I wonder if maybe I'm more pissed about it than you are."

"You might be," Kate said, already thinking of visiting the hospital to see Melissa and Michelle sometime after breakfast.

"You want me to stop calling you?" DeMarco asked.

"No, of course not. I appreciate it. I just don't want you to feel that you owe it to me."

"Look, if we aren't going to be partners, I'd like to consider you a friend," DeMarco said. "And that's hard for me to say. So yes…as a common courtesy, I'm going to keep you updated."

"In that case, I look forward to your call. Best of luck out there, Agent DeMarco."

Kate ended the call and made herself the day's first cup of coffee. She sipped at it while watching the news, wondering if she'd make breakfast herself or grab some on the way to the hospital. *These are the kinds of important decisions I have to make while retired,* she thought grimly.

It was wild to think of just how fast-paced yesterday had been. Compared to the humdrum state of this morning, it was almost surreal.

When her phone rang again, she was expecting it to be DeMarco. Maybe she had finally met the new agents and wanted to complain about them. Or maybe the print from the shower door had come back and—

But there was no name on the display of her phone, just a number she did not recognize. She answered it hesitantly. She'd never trusted calls from numbers that weren't programmed into her phone—a lesson she'd learned in her life inside *and* outside of the bureau.

"Hello?" she asked.

"Is this Agent Wise?" a man's voice asked.

She nearly corrected the man to inform him that the "agent" in front of her name was no longer accurate. But she said nothing, curious to see what the call was about.

"Yes, this is Agent Wise," she said, not minding the minor lie.

"This is Daryl Woodward," he said. "Chief Budd gave me your number last night and I remember you told me to call you if I thought of anything else."

The safe and wise thing to do would have been to stop him right there and redirect him to DeMarco. But then there was the steadfast agent still residing over her, a part of her that not only did not want to extend the process any longer for Daryl Woodward, but also wanted to see if she could do anything at all to help with the case that wouldn't get her scolded later down the line.

"Did you come up with something?" she asked.

"Maybe. You asked if they were all involved in anything together, like a club or group or something. I'm pretty sure they were all part of this class at the gym. To be sure, I checked Taylor's planner. She had the class every Monday, Wednesday, and Friday at four in the afternoon. She would have been coming back from it last night. I…well, a while back I found some text messages on her phone between her and her friends. Group texts, you know? They were talking about the class. Julie and Wendy got a little raunchy about the instructor."

"By raunchy, do you mean sexually suggestive?"

"As in Julie mentioned licking the sweat off of his chest. But somewhere in there, Wendy also mentioned how the guy was sort of a douchebag. There was a lot of suggestive talk and I think Lacy might even have slept with him. I don't know. I'm not proud of it, but I took pictures of the conversations, just in case Taylor ever deleted them. I wanted them as proof that her friends were nothing but trouble. I can send you the conversation if you'd like."

"That would be great. And do you happen to know the name of the class and the instructor?"

"It's all in the thread," Daryl said. "I'll send the pictures over to you as soon as we get off of here. The class was at New You Fitness. You know where it is?"

"I do," Kate said. "Thanks for this. This could potentially bring up a lead."

Daryl sounded hopeful when he ended the call. Kate wasn't sure if it would bring up a lead or not, but if the messages were as suggestive as he was letting on, then it could be very helpful indeed.

True to his word, Daryl sent the text thread over within a few minutes. He sent it as a series of screenshots which Kate read while drinking her coffee. She read it all, noting some of the more surprising comments. Line by line, she became more and more certain that she did indeed have a lead at her fingertips. The messages were from two weeks ago, making it seem as if she were reading the final thoughts of ghosts.

Anyone else have dirty dreams of Julio last night? Julie had asked the group.

My-God, Lacy said. *I didn't even wait to sleep. I went to the bedside drawer and utilized some hardware while Peter was asleep. Good dreams?*

Yeah. I was licking the sweat off of his chest, Julie said. *Tasted like wine.*

Weirdo, Wendy said.

That man IS fine, Taylor replied. *I'd keep going to cycling class until my joints got old and busted if he'd keep teaching.*

Speaking of joints, how'd he treat your knees, Lacy? Wendy asked.

They still sting, but GOD it was worth it. He texted me later and said he's keeping my panties in his gym bag as a reminder.

Says it turns him on. He's good at pretending it didn't happen, but the way he was looking at me yesterday...

Stop it, Julie said. *Or I'm going to get MY hardware.*

That big one? Wendy asked. *I can hear that fucking thing all the way over here at my house.*

The messages went on from there, but that was the section that Kate honed in on. It did seem to suggest that Lacy had, at some point, slept with the instructor of their cycling class.

Looks like Lacy was seeing someone on the side while her husband did his own thing after all, Kate thought.

And just like that, she had a lead.

The only question that remained was whether or not she could pass it off to DeMarco and remain uninvolved.

The answer, of course, was no. She smiled as she called up DeMarco. The younger agent answered right away. "I thought I was supposed to be calling you," DeMarco said.

"Well, I got something. How long before those other agents show up?"

"About an hour, I guess."

"Okay. Meet me at your motel in twenty minutes. I might have something."

"Like what?"

Already headed out the door, Kate relayed her conversation with Daryl Woodward and the text thread he had sent her. With a sudden change to the morning's schedule, it looked like she'd be picking up breakfast on her way out after all.

CHAPTER THIRTY THREE

The early morning crowd was thin at New You Fitness. A few people were using the treadmills and only a handful of others were scattered around the various stations. Kate could see all of this from the front desk, as the gym area was visible through clear Plexiglas to the left of the desk. The place was a little too small to be considered an actual gym but it was also much cleaner than a typical gym.

With DeMarco at her side, Kate approached the desk. A young woman who was likely a part-timer with college classes in between looked up at them with a smile. "How can I help you ladies this morning?"

"We're looking for a man named Julio Almas," DeMarco said. "Your website says he's the instructor for cycling classes and Keto workouts."

"Oh, sure," the young woman said. "He should be back in Room Six. He's got a Keto class starting in about twenty minutes."

The agents nodded their thanks and headed around the desk where a thin corridor housed several private rooms. On the drive to the fitness center, they had discussed the best approach to take. It was agreed that DeMarco would take the lead just in case things got out of hand. The fewer chances Kate had to reveal that she was not an active agent—or to lie about it, for that matter—the better.

They came to Room 6 and found only one man inside. He was laying out several mats on the floor, getting ready for his next class apparently. DeMarco knocked on the door and walked inside, not waiting for the man to respond.

He turned to face them and Kate saw right away why Julio might be the subject of needy women's fantasies. He was of average height but was built like a Greek statue. His pecs and abs were just about visible through the tight tank top he wore. His long black hair was slicked back in what kids were now calling a "man-bun." He had dark eyes that were instantly captivating and every feature on his face seemed to complement everything else. To say the man was handsome was an understatement. Kate couldn't help but wonder if he had been hired to get more women to sign up for private classes.

She also wondered whether, if Lacy *had* been sleeping with him—even just the one time—if she was the only one.

"Need some help?" Julio asked.

"Yes, in fact," DeMarco said, keeping her cool. "We'd like to speak with you about a few recent participants in one of your cycling classes." She showed her ID and introduced herself. Kate watched him closely and saw a flicker of fear in his eyes. It was the first time since walking into the crime scene at Julie Hicks's house that she thought they might have something here.

"You mean Mrs. Hicks and Mrs. Thurmond, right?"

"And you know that how, exactly?" DeMarco asked.

"Word gets around. It's terrible. They were both murdered, is that right?"

"That's exactly right," Kate said. "Another of your members was killed last night as well. Taylor Woodward."

He seemed legitimately shocked, but there still seemed to be something off about him.

"We're here because your cycling class seems to be the one thing that linked them together aside from the occasional wine drinking session and hanging out at the pool. Do you know if they had any relationships established with your other students?"

"I can't say for sure. I don't know. I really didn't know them that well. Just enough to say hello when they came into class."

"You sure about that?" Kate asked. "You didn't know Lacy Thurmond any better than your other students?"

The question rocked him and if he tried at all to hide it, he failed miserably. "I...I don't understand why you're here," he said. He was looking around the room like a caged animal seeking a way out.

"Did you have any sort of physical relationship with Lacy, Taylor, or Julie?"

He nodded his head nervously. "Yes. I did. I slept with Lacy. But it was just one time. We were planning on a second but then I heard about what happened and..."

"Was the sex mutual?" DeMarco asked.

"Yes."

"How did it happen?" DeMarco asked.

"I'm not comfortable with this line of questioning," Julio said.

"Okay then," DeMarco asked. "Was it in her home?"

"No. It was here, actually. In the changing room after one of my shifts."

"And did you keep a souvenir?" Kate asked.

It was clear that Julio was truly shocked now. He shook his head violently as his bottom lip started to tremble.

"Please just tell the truth," Kate said. "You are in no trouble for hooking up with a married woman. We just need a better idea of how she spent her last few days before she was murdered."

"I...I have the underwear she was wearing. They're in my gym bag."

"Is that all?" Kate asked.

"Yes. You have my word."

"Where is that gym bag?" DeMarco said. "Let us have a look inside and we might be able to get out of your hair before your next class starts."

"No, no...you need a warrant, right?"

"If you choose to go that route, yes," Kate said. "But then we can go get it and make sure to come visit you again with that warrant right in the middle of one of your classes. So really, it's your choice."

Julio looked angry now but he started walking toward the door, waving him on behind him. He led them to the end of the hallway, to a room with a decorative sign that read STAFF ONLY. The room was a small one, boasting only a single table, several chairs, and an entire back wall of small lockers. He went to the one with his name marked on a piece of masking tape and popped it open.

"Here," he said, throwing a well-worn gym bag onto the table. He was clearly pissed off but was more driven by his need to get them out of there before his next class.

Kate stopped herself from stepping forward, reminding herself that DeMarco had to take the lead today. She could only imagine the look on Duran's face if he knew she was taking part in this. She nodded to DeMarco and the younger agent unzipped the bag. She rummaged around for a few moments and then, seemingly for no reason, yanked her hand back.

Kate, DeMarco, and Julio stood in a tight group, in silence. Kate locked eyes with DeMarco, trying to figure out what was wrong—what had happened to cause DeMarco to pull her hand away so quickly.

And then she saw the blood on the side of DeMarco's hand.

"What the hell?" Julio said, taking a cautious step forward.

DeMarco's hand went to her sidearm as she wheeled around on him. "Don't move," she said. "Stay right there. One more step forward and I *will* draw my gun."

Kate stepped forward, closer to the bag. She peered inside as, undaunted, DeMarco reached back inside. This time when

DeMarco's hand came out, she brought a pair of white lace panties with her. The white of the material made the dark red of the blood stand out.

The blood was not brand new, but it was fresh enough to stick to DeMarco's skin. DeMarco looked inside and then back to Kate. "Have a look," she said.

Kate looked into the bag. She saw Julio's gym shorts, his wallet, and a pair of black gloves. The gloves had more blood on them, as did the nylon bottom of the bag. Like the blood on the panties and DeMarco's hand, it was still relatively new.

"Against the wall," DeMarco said, facing back toward Julio.

"I don't understand," he said. "What the hell is going on?"

"You're under arrest," DeMarco said. "If these are indeed Lacy Thurmond's underwear, you've got a ton of explaining to do. And this blood is fresh...not Lacy's but maybe from someone else you've seen recently?"

"The panties are Lacy's, yes. But I have no idea where the blood came from!"

"You can recite all of that in an interrogation room," DeMarco said as she took out her set of cuffs and applied them to Julio's wrists.

"What the *fuck*?" Julio yelled.

Kate looked back into the bag. The blood wasn't exactly pooled up, but there was enough of it to be glistening. She looked for any sign of a weapon, but there was none.

Seems almost too perfect, she thought. *Of course, if this last murder was based on passion and he maybe felt a sense of finality or accomplishment, maybe he got lazy in his clean-up.*

With Julio still facing the lockers and his arms cuffed behind his back, DeMarco looked back to Kate. "What now?" she asked. It seemed like a loaded question but Kate knew what she meant. If she wasn't supposed to be on the case, how should they proceed?

But there was the blood and the panties...an admitted affair to top it all off. Kate was pretty sure she could make the call and be in the clear.

"I'll start by calling Budd," she said. "And then I'll call Duran."

"You sure?" DeMarco asked.

The truth was, she *wasn't* sure. But she went ahead and placed the first call to Budd before she could lose her nerve.

CHAPTER THIRTY FOUR

An hour and fifteen minutes later, Kate was waiting outside of the interrogation room in Chief Budd's precinct. The last hour had been a particularly active one. First of all, there had been the small swarm of policemen who had come to New You Fitness to apprehend Julio. At about the same time, the two agents had arrived from DC to assist DeMarco. They were understandably pissed off to find that the case seemed to already be wrapped up. They waited outside of the interrogation room, too.

It was killing Kate not to partake in the questioning. But when she had called Duran to update him, he had been irate. Kate had expected him to be a little upset, but not as angry as he appeared to be through the phone. As a form of punishment, he'd ordered her to let DeMarco handle the interrogation and that she, Kate, was not to even watch through any sort of surveillance or monitors within the interrogation room.

He had, however, ended the call with a word of thanks for apprehending the man who seemed to be the killer. Even after being scolded, Kate couldn't help but smile. It had been a rocky start, but her first case after coming back had finally wrapped up.

Or had it?

She continued to feel that finding the panties and the blood had seemed too easy. Julio had even admitted to having the panties in his gym bag—but the blood had seemed to throw him off. If she was in the interrogation room, she thought she might be able to read his expressions. She hadn't been sure if the look on his face was a fear borne of guilt or of genuine shock at seeing the blood.

As she waited outside the room, Chief Budd came walking toward her from the front of the building. The two new agents from DC were walking in the other direction, looking to interview some of Julio's co-workers. As for Budd, Kate was pretty sure he'd been with his PR people, drumming up a draft of a press release. It seemed that they were already pretty sure they had their guy. And while even Kate had to admit that it certainly *looked* that way, something was nagging at her.

It's just too damned easy, she thought.

Budd approached her with a grin and extended his hand for a shake. "I understand you're in some hot water with your supervisor," he said. "That's none of my business and quite frankly, I don't care. I just wanted to thank you for cracking this thing. One more murder in that neighborhood and this place would have turned into a madhouse."

She was about to respond to him when the door to the interrogation room opened. DeMarco came out, looking mostly satisfied but a little troubled. Kate looked at her watch and saw that DeMarco had been in there for twenty minutes.

"What's your initial reaction?" Kate asked.

"Everything points to it being him," she said. "The time lines up. There's the sexual relationship to be considered. The blood in his bag…"

"And the gloves," Kate said. "It would explain why we weren't able to find any prints at the crime scenes. Does he have an alibi for between six and seven yesterday afternoon?"

"No. He says he left work, stopped at a WaWa for gas and to grab a snack. Says traffic was pretty bad so it took him a while."

"So you think it's him?" Kate asked.

"Like I said…it *seems* like it. Just the way he responded to me when I described the crime scene…he looked disgusted."

"You have to get that blood tested as soon as possible," Kate said. "And see if you can get some DNA off of the gloves. We should know with certainty if he's the killer within twelve hours."

"Seems like a lot of work to me," Budd said. "As far as I'm concerned, this case is closed. Damned good work, ladies." And with that, he gave them a little bow of appreciation and headed back the way he came.

"Duran feels the same way," DeMarco told Kate when Budd was gone. "He texted while I was in there. He wants me back in DC tonight. The two new agents are to stay here and run clean-up."

"How do you feel about that?" Kate asked.

"Weird. I don't know…it feels too…too…"

"Easy?"

"Exactly," DeMarco said.

They both looked back at the closed interrogation room door and didn't say a word. Their tense silence, though, spoke volumes.

CHAPTER THIRTY FIVE

Kate knew better than to go against Duran's wishes again. But at the same time, she could not just let the case rest if she felt it was still active—especially while local law enforcement was practically celebrating that it was seemingly closed.

So she met in the middle. She returned to her house after DeMarco started filling out the necessary paperwork at the police precinct. But she took her case files with her. She was wondering if she could find something that linked to Julio now that they at least had a profile to work from.

She threw a sandwich together and ate it at the kitchen table with the notes out in front of her. But no matter where she looked, she could find nothing that tied in to the personality Julio exhibited. She supposed it might come down to forensics—the slashing motions of the wounds in relation to Julio's strength, hand preference, and so on. That, or the blood in his bag would indeed turn out to belong to Taylor Woodward and then that would be that. It would take a miracle for him to not be convicted of murder.

Kate pored over the same files she'd already scrutinized several times and found nothing new. She even pulled out the small stack of medical records that Budd's men had pulled in the aftermath of the Thurmond case. Before being taken to her grandparents', the daughter had spent a little time with the Department of Social Services. From what Kate could tell, they had requested the medical records—a standard practice if they weren't immediately sure how long a child would be in their care.

Kate scanned these documents, sure that nothing would be there. She saw where Peter Thurmond had gone to the doctor two years ago for prostatitis. The daughter, Olivia, had gone a few months ago for what turned out to be strep throat. And it was there that Kate saw something she had missed before. It was small and insignificant but was still *something.*

Let it go, she told herself. *Duran doesn't want you on this anymore. He thinks you've already caught the killer. Stop grasping at straws.*

Of course, Kate rarely took her own advice. She looked to the very small detail both she and DeMarco had overlooked. Underneath "Emergency Contacts" on Olivia's form, there were two names and titles. One was *Peter Thurmond – father.* The other read *Pamela Duncan – part-time nanny.*

Well, that's new, Kate thought. She looked at the number beside Pamela Duncan's name and wasted no time. Before fully thinking things through, she called it.

Are you trying *to get yourself in trouble?* she asked herself.

She had no time to come up with an answer. The phone was answered just after the first ring. "Hello?"

"Hi, is this Pamela Duncan?"

"It is."

"Hi, my name is Kate Wise. I'm a consultant with the FBI." A lie, sure…but not as bad as stating that she was still an active agent. "I saw in some of our background information that you are listed on Olivia Thurmond's medical records as an emergency contact. Were you a nanny for the Thurmond family?"

"Every now and then, yes. Have you found who killed Lacy yet?"

"There is currently a suspect in custody but nothing is definitive yet. Ms. Duncan, I was wondering if you might be able to shed some light on what Lacy's life was like. Maybe even the lives of some of her friends, too."

"Have you talked to them yet? Lacy's friends?"

"Yes. Her closest friends, anyway."

Pamela hesitated for a moment before asking: "Where are you calling from, Ms. Wise?"

"I'm in Richmond. Your phone number indicates that you are, too."

"Can you meet me in about an hour?" Pamela asked.

Kate found the request a little strange but she wasn't about to turn down the opportunity. That old agent instinct was raising its head and sniffing the air. It seemed like there might be something there.

"Just tell me the place," Kate said.

Pamela did, and Kate was back out the door fifteen minutes later.

CHAPTER THIRTY SIX

They met at one of Kate's favorite little spots in Carytown, a place called the Galaxy Diner. It was the kind of trendy place that served fried pickles as well as gluten-free options. When Pamela Duncan took the seat across the table from Kate, she did not look nervous and reserved, as Kate had been expecting. Instead, she looked almost pleased to be there. She even smiled warmly at Kate as she sat down.

After a brief round of introductions, Kate wasted no time in getting to the center of the matter.

"How long did you work for the Thurmonds?" she asked.

"About eight months," Pamela said.

"And what sort of work did you do? I ask only because I find it odd that a mother and wife that stayed at home most of the time would need a nanny."

"Well, about a year or so ago, from what I understand, Lacy had strongly considered going back to college. Some online courses, maybe a few classes at the community college. She'd had everything ready to go when I was hired. I was brought on to mainly just pick Olivia up from school, tidy up the house, prepare dinner. That sort of thing. I only worked about fifteen hours a week—twenty on busy weeks. And even when the college thing didn't pan out, they kept me on for a few weeks. When they let me go, it was amicable. But they did ask if they could keep me in their contacts to call on me every now and then, and I agreed."

"How long ago since they let you go?"

"About five months ago."

"And did they ever call on your services afterwards?"

"A few times. Lacy never actually came out and said as much, but I got the feeling that she and her husband were having some rough patches. They planned these weekend getaways to try to work on their marriage. But as far as I could tell, Peter was cheating on her. He wasn't very good at hiding it, either."

"They apparently trusted you, right?" Kate asked. "You were put down on the medical records as Olivia's emergency contact. Given that, why did you feel the need to speak with me in person?"

"Because Lacy's really close friends...they were trouble, you know? They seemed like such sweet, beautiful women when I first met them. I'd see them here and there, coming to the house. I was there one day when all of them were sitting around the dining room, drinking wine. I don't remember all of their names but there was one that openly admitted to cheating on her husband. And the others seemed to encourage it. It didn't seem right, you know?

"But there's something else…something that never sat right with me. And it's sitting heavy on me now because of the murders."

"What is it?" Kate asked. "Ms. Duncan, if you have something that you think might seem like a stretch, it could help. We do have a suspect currently in custody but nothing is set in stone yet."

"The woman that died yesterday…last name was Woodward, right?"

"That's correct."

"Well, there was this one time that the husband—Daryl, I think his name is—came by the Thurmond home. He was looking for his wife, Taylor. He was really worried about her. Given that group of friends, I don't blame him. He said he knew she was in some kind of trouble."

"Did Lacy ever tell her husband about the incident?"

"No. I think she was scared to. Whatever trouble the Woodward woman was in, I think all of the women might have been wrapped up in it. Her husband was worried sick about her."

"How long ago was this?" Kate asked.

"Maybe two months. Lacy had called me to pick Olivia up from school and take her to cheerleading practice. It's fortunate that I even stopped by the house. I wanted to check in to see how things were going with Lacy."

Kate thought back to the previous night, of how Daryl had been drowning in his grief. Usually spouses behaved that way when they felt they hadn't done enough to stop the murder. Daryl must have suspected all along that Julio was the killer. And now he was too ashamed to say, as he didn't act on his instincts and prevent it in time.

"Daryl was so worried about her, like to the point of almost crying in front of me. And then, two months later, she's dead," she added.

Kate finally felt certain: Julio was the killer, indeed. And now all she needed was for Daryl to confirm it, to tell her the entire story of exactly the type of man that Julio was.

***

154

Throughout the course of her career, Kate had come to firmly believe in the old saying *"When it rains, it pours."* Her first little drizzle had come from the meeting with Pamela Duncan.

Her next drizzle came when her phone rang as she was headed back toward Amber Hills. She picked it up right away, not even bothering to check the caller display. "This is Wise," she said, careful not to use the agent moniker.

"Agent Wise, this is Robert Smith from the coroner's office. While we didn't find anything conclusive on the body of Taylor Woodward, there was one detail I thought you might find interesting."

"I'll take whatever I can get," Kate said.

She wondered why he was calling her but then assumed he had no way of knowing that she had been taken off the case.

"The punch to the face left a very small bruise, leading me to believe that it was more of a jab—almost a playful one—than a powerful punch meant to severely hurt the victim. From the punch alone, there are two things that I believe we can determine. First of all, given the placement and the angle, I think it's safe to say that the killer is left-handed. Of course, any number of elements could prove me wrong but it seems very likely."

"And the second thing?" Kate asked.

"There are no prints, indicating the killer wore gloves. However, there is a small indentation along the bruise. It's barely visible at all to the naked eye but under the right lighting and magnification, it's there: a shape that suggests the killer wears a ring on his left hand. Probably either the ring finger or pinky."

"And if he's throwing punches, the pinky wouldn't leave much of an imprint, would it?"

"Likely not."

"A ring on the left ring finger," Kate said. "So the killer was married?"

"I'd say that's a safe bet," Smith said.

Julio, she knew, wore a wedding ring. *And* a pinky ring.

"Thanks for this," Kate said. She got a warm fuzzy feeling in her gut and her heart started pumping a bit faster. She ended the call and immediately pulled up DeMarco's number.

She answered after three rings. DeMarco sounded irritated and a bit tired. "Hey, Wise," she said. "If you're calling for updates, there are none. Duran and the local PD are hanging on the assumption that Julio Almas is our guy."

"Well, I just got a call from the coroner with an early report on Taylor Woodward's body. So tell me something…is Julio right-handed or left-handed?"

"I'm actually not sure. I never bothered looking."

"You still at the PD?"

"Unfortunately."

"Find some bullshit form and take it in there for him to sign. Tell him he'll be released soon after. Pay attention to which hand he signs with."

"Okay…" DeMarco said, a hint of intrigue in her voice. "Give me a second."

"I'll hold."

Kate listened to the sound of movement from DeMarco's end. She heard the faint voices of the policemen in the background, the place still in a bit of an uproar from the morning's excitement. She was ready to put to rest her doubts about Julio Almas.

Three minutes passed. She was ten minutes away from the gates an Amber Hills when DeMarco came back on the phone.

"He signed it," DeMarco said. "He's a lefty. Why? What have you got?"

Kate sighed.

"Nothing," she said. "Just bad instincts, I guess. Or worn-out ones. Maybe there is a wisdom in retiring at 55. You've got your man. It's Julio."

She hung up and sighed. Maybe she was getting too old for this.

It was time to put all this to bed, once and for all. To find out the entire truth about Julio. And Daryl, she suspected, held the key.

CHAPTER THIRTY SEVEN

Kate wondered if Daryl was able to bring himself to go back home after the murder of his wife. There was no real timetable for grief; some would wait weeks before returning to the home where a loved one was killed while others had no problem with returning right away.

When she pulled up in front of the house, she saw Daryl's mother sitting in a rocker on the front porch. She eyed Kate when she got out of the car and started up the sidewalk.

"Hello again," Kate said as pleasantly as she could. "Is Daryl home?"

"He is," the mother said. "But he's very tired and understandably upset."

"I understand," Kate said. She approached the porch and slowly climbed the stairs. She then spoke in a low conspiratorial voice, hoping to sway the old woman. "This is not public knowledge yet, but we have a potential suspect in custody," she said. "If I could speak with him in private for no more than ten minutes, it could help us ensure that we do indeed have the right man."

Daryl's mother seemed happy at the news, nodding her appreciation. "Okay," she said. "He'd like that, I think. He feels helpless right now. Maybe this will give him a sense of purpose. Would you please let him know I'm going to run to the pharmacy to pick up my prescription?"

"Yes ma'am."

Kate entered the house at the same time Daryl's mother walked to the car in the driveway. As the screen door closed behind Kate, she could hear Mrs. Woodward's car cranking to life.

"Excuse me?" Kate called out. "Mr. Woodward? It's Kate Wise again. Your mother said it was okay if I come inside."

"Of course," he called out from elsewhere in the house. "I'm back in the kitchen."

Kate followed the sound of his voice through the foyer and down the small hallway. The house had a mostly open floor plan so she was able to see the kitchen immediately. She saw Daryl arranging pastries and bagels on the counter. They were still in boxes, some of the pastries still steaming.

"Sorry to bother you again," she said. "But I wanted you to know that we checked up on the cycling instructor. We found enough evidence to take him in."

"It was him?" Daryl asked.

"We don't know for sure, but we're looking into it right now. Looks like it could be a strong possibility. I hope you understand that even as the husband of a recent victim, we can't give you the strict details until an official arrest has been made."

"I understand," he said.

"In the meantime, I was hoping you might be able to help me out. We were told you were very worried about your wife at one point. Why was that?"

He frowned. She watched as his shoulders slumped and he slowly withdrew.

He remained silent.

"Mr. Woodward," she pressed on, "I know this is difficult. I know you don't want to implicate your wife in anything that may have been...unseemly. But, however concerning or embarrassing it may be, I need to know. We have a man locked up right now who may or may not be the right suspect. And I suspect that you may know of some difficulty your wife was in, some difficulty that may help us know for certain if we have the killer."

He stared back at her, his eyes dull and vacant, and opened his mouth to speak several times.

But each time, he remained silent, as if he couldn't bring himself to say it.

But there was more to it than that.

As she observed him closely, she noticed, just for a fraction of an instant, a flicker in his eye. It was something that made no sense. It wasn't one of recognition.

It was one of rage.

It came, and then it left as soon as it did—so fast that she wasn't even sure whether she saw it or imagined it.

Suddenly, her heart started to pound wildly.

No, she thought. *It can't be him.*

But could it?

She thought suddenly of what Tate O'Brien had said about murders committed in the acts of both rage and love.

Several wives were killed. Not just his. If he had killed his wife, that meant...he would have killed all of them.

But why? Why kill all the wives if he only wanted his own dead?

It couldn't be, she thought. *Could it?*

158

Were all those murders just to cover up his trail? To make this seem like a serial killer? To deflect attention from the real wife he wanted dead? From himself as a suspect?

To create the perfect murder?

"Did you hear me, Agent Wise?"

Kate snapped out of it, back to the present. She found Daryl staring at her questioningly. Her mind spun, and she felt light-headed, wondering if she could be standing a few feet from the killer.

"I'm sorry," she said, her voice trembling, trying to keep it calm. "I wasn't listening."

"I asked you if there was anything else I could help you with?" he asked, his voice so calm that she wondered if she had imagined the whole thing.

His hand, she thought fast. *Get him to write something. See if he's a lefty.*

She cleared her throat and tried to keep her voice calm.

"Yes," she said. "There is just one more thing. Could you perhaps give me the names of a few friends that Taylor hung out with?"

"OK," he said with a frown. "Want me to text them to you?"

"I'm old-school," she said as gently as possible. "Could you just write them down?"

He eyed her suspiciously, seemed to hesitate.

Finally, he turned and walked to the left side of the kitchen and opened up a drawer. He took out a pen and a Post-It.

He started writing.

With his left hand.

As his wedding band shone dully from his ring finger.

Stay calm, she told herself. *This still doesn't prove anything. You have to goad him. It's now or never. You can't walk out without knowing for sure.*

"I spoke with your mother out front," Kate said. "She wanted me to tell you she was going to run to the pharmacy." She paused a beat and then added: "Are you close to your mother?"

There it was again. The flicker of rage in his eyes, this time recognizable, and stronger.

And that was when Kate knew for sure. Many killers she had dealt with had been oppressed by their mothers in some way or another; too many times that had been the trigger to vent their feelings.

Daryl just gritted his jaw and stared back, the hostility pouring through his face.

"What business is that of yours?" he asked.

He sneered at her slightly and then turned his head. He walked to the coffeemaker and started pouring himself a cup of coffee. His hand was visibly trembling.

She didn't wait for him. She knew it was now or never. She knew she should leave the house, call for backup.

But she just couldn't bring herself to.

Her entire career, she just couldn't bring herself to. She always had to push it, just a little too far. Always had to disregard that voice of caution.

"Mr. Woodward, the coroner is all but certain that your wife was punched by a lefty—a lefty wearing a ring on his left ring finger," she said. "Julio Almas is right-handed and has no rings," she lied. "Why do you think that is?"

Daryl Woodward stopped for a moment, in the midst of bringing his coffee cup to his mouth. His back was mostly to her but she could see from the posture in his shoulders that he was taking a defensive position.

"*You're* a lefty, aren't you?" she asked.

He tensed up, his back still to her.

"You're insane," he muttered, his voice growing darker.

Now, she told herself. *Stop now and call for backup.*

She knew she should. But she just couldn't. She had to finish this thing. On her own.

"You hated the other women but didn't really want to kill them, did you? You really truly only wanted Taylor dead. But how could you kill her and not have the cops suspect you? Easy. You kill a few other wives and make it look like a serial. That way, a lone husband wouldn't so clearly be a suspect.

"But you went a little too far with your wife, Daryl. That was a murder of passion. The only one."

He turned around and smiled at her, as if impressed.

Then he charged.

Kate threw her arms up to defend herself, fully prepared to catch his left arm—which he was leading with—and whip him over onto the floor.

But she did not expect the hot coffee thrown at her. It splashed against her face, getting into her eyes. It was very hot, but not freshly hot. Still, the sting of it was enough to take her off guard.

Daryl threw his full weight into her. Her back slammed against the kitchen island behind her and as she recoiled and fell to the floor with her back spasming, she felt the first punch fall, splitting open her lip.

Blood flowed, instantly filling Kate's mouth. Just as she tasted it, thick and coppery on her tongue, he planted a knee in her stomach. The wind went rushing out of her and for the first time since entering the FBI, she allowed herself to think:

This is it. This is how I'm going to die.

CHAPTER THIRTY EIGHT

Had the coffee been freshly brewed and piping hot, Kate would have been in much worse shape. As it was, she was more concerned with her back. She'd hit the edge of the island hard and something back there was going numb. Meanwhile, Daryl had her pinned to the floor, a knee in her stomach and both of his hands on her shoulders.

"I wish I had the knife I killed those bitches with," Daryl said. "I'd slit you open right here, right now. And it would be a shame because you're not like them. They deserved it, you know?"

Good, she thought. *This idiot is going to brag on himself. He's strong and easily overpowers me, but the longer he keeps me here, in this position, the better chance I have of escaping.*

"It wasn't a mistake that I started with Julie. She's a…well, she *was* such a tease. We were sleeping with each other. Had been for months. Taylor didn't know, though. She was too hung up on her own little activities. And yes, I knew all about the cycling instructor. He's slept with half the fucking neighborhood. So yeah…why not pin it on him?"

He smiled and a chuckle escaped from his lips. It was this one little cocky action that gave Kate the opening she needed. As his right hand relaxed with his laughter, she pushed forward, sitting up and using her right shoulder to force the weight of the movement. She then threw her elbow up and out, catching him in the chin. She heard the sharp *click* of his teeth smashing together.

He tottered back, shocked, and nearly fell off of her. Enraged, he threw another punch downward. She caught him by the wrist, twisted hard to the left, and his entire body followed suit. Had he not struck the side of the kitchen island, she would have been able to apply an arm bar, ripping his elbow out of its socket and ending the fight there.

But the island was in the way. As she scrambled to her feet, Daryl opened a nearby cabinet. Kate was so confused by the action that she didn't see the rolling pin until it was too late. She swayed backward but the end of it still clipped her on the side of the head. She spun around as little black stars swirled across her field of vision.

He came at her again, the rolling pin raised like a club.

No, Kate thought with a maniacal sort of panic. *Not like this. Hell no...*

He swung the pin again, straight across this time. Kate managed to block it with her left forearm. A bolt of pain rocketed up her arm. She cried out, looking around for a weapon to use. So far, she'd been burned by coffee and struck with a rolling pin. She'd be damned if she'd be insulted any farther.

She backed up against the kitchen sink and found a fork sitting in the edge. It was positioned on a plate with what looked like the remnants of scrambled eggs. As Daryl surged forward one more time, she grabbed it and jabbed forward in a move that reminded her of her younger days. She moved with the speed of a seasoned boxer, and the prongs of the fork tore into Daryl's left cheek before she yanked it back out.

He screamed, dropping the rolling pin and barreling forward. "Bitch!" he yelled. "I'll kill you, too. Then Wendy Hudson, then I'll be done with all of them!" He let out a roar of rage as he collided with her. She jammed the fork into his right shoulder, the prongs completely buried. She left it there. He howled again but kept coming. He rammed her hard against the edge of the sink once, twice...the numbness in her back was spreading. She was afraid it might make her collapse. And if she hit the ground again...

"They all teased me, even Julie," he went on. "Even during the affair, she'd threaten to tell Taylor if I didn't do certain things. They're all controlling...every single one of them. Flirting. Showing skin. Making me weak...they—"

Kate took advantage of his moment of weakness. She drove her knee up into his stomach. He hunched over and when he did, Kate brought her right hand down in hard downward jab. She clipped his chin and sent him to the floor.

On the way down, he grabbed her shirt. Had it not been a to-the-death sort of fight, it might have seemed like he was trying to grab her breast. He yanked down and she fought against it, bringing her knee hard into his chest. They fell in a heap of legs and arms, fighting for control against the side of the sink.

"Freeze!"

The shout came out of nowhere. Both Kate and Daryl turned toward the direction of the voice. Through blurred vision, Kate saw DeMarco standing at the entrance to the kitchen.

"Get off of her," DeMarco said.

Daryl responded right away. He raised his hands and backed off. He took a stumbling step away and then slowly turned to face

DeMarco. The fork was still in his shoulder, standing as rigid as a beam in the ground.

"On your knees, hands behind your back," DeMarco ordered.

"You don't understand," he said as he obeyed her orders. "They were evil. They were using me. Unfaithful. Deranged. They *loved* to have men look at them...even at the pool, even those teenage kids..."

"You okay, Wise?" DeMarco asked, ignoring him.

Kate only nodded. Her back was a knot of nothingness, the numbness no longer spreading but seeming to centralize. The black stars were still in her vision and she was pretty sure the side of her head that had caught the rolling pin was swelling. She leaned against the sink, watching DeMarco as she moved around behind Daryl.

She saw Daryl moving before DeMarco did, her attention on her wounded partner.

Kate yelled a warning and the next few seconds seemed to explode into motion.

Daryl moved with the energy and desperation of a trapped man. In a motion that was so morbid it was nearly comical, he yanked the fork out of his shoulder and plunged it into DeMarco's leg. When she buckled and let out a scream, Daryl instantly went for her right hand. He sank his teeth into her wrist and yanked her hard by the arm.

She dropped the gun in her surprise and the moment it hit the floor, he went for it.

Kate raced forward, hoping her numb back would simply remember what it was supposed to do. She noticed that DeMarco was now on her knees, clutching her wrist. She was losing a hell of a lot of blood.

But Kate had to look beyond that. Daryl's hand was on the gun. His fingers were closing around it...

Kate brought her right knee up, connecting squarely with his face. There was a crunch as his nose shattered. He reeled back, dazed. His eyes swam and blood came gushing out of his nose. Kate retrieved the gun and kept it pointed at him. Her arms were trembling and she did everything she could not to just pull the trigger.

"DeMarco...how are you?"

"Bloody."

Still, she got to her feet and came forward, still clutching her bitten wrist. She yanked a dish towel from the handle of the oven door and wrapped it around her wrist. She then expertly put handcuffs on a nearly comatose Daryl Woodward. When she had them secured, she let him go. He took a single stumbling step forward and then fell face down on the floor.

The two women looked at one another in stunned silence. Kate could not remember the last time she'd taken such a beating. But that concern was secondary to what she saw in DeMarco. The younger agent was stumbling, having to catch the kitchen counter for balance. The dish towel she had laced around her wrist was pretty much soaked through with blood. Daryl had apparently bitten deep, perhaps nicking an artery.

"Stay with me, okay?" she told DeMarco. She pulled out her phone and dialed 911.

"Yeah," DeMarco said with a sleepy smile. "Not going anywhere."

She even managed a nervous little laugh before her eyes closed and she fell to the floor right beside Daryl Woodward.

CHAPTER THIRTY NINE

Kate found herself sitting in Duran's office for the second time in a week. This time, things weren't quite as cordial, though. DeMarco was sitting next to her and it was apparent that she was not used to being scolded. It was also apparent that she was not used to being injured. She'd received two shots and twenty-six stitches due to Daryl Woodward's bite. She'd lost a lot of blood but had been stable the entire time, as soon as the ambulance had arrived.

As for Kate, she was sore. The fight with Woodward had taken it out of her. It was proof of just how unconditioned she was these days. And it was more than not working out like she once had. It was age—something she had no say about.

Duran had just read them the riot act for going into Daryl Woodward's house two days ago. He was more aggravated about their direct disobedience than the fact that they had both been injured and had ended up nearly killing a man.

Their saving grace came in a series of audio recordings on Daryl's phone. He'd kept a record of the comings and goings of Julie and Lacy. The recordings went back over the course of over two months. He'd call them degrading names while he narrated their schedules. One particular recording had gone into great detail about a recent tryst with Julie. The description of a tattoo on her inner thigh basically sealed the case for them.

"So here's my conundrum," Duran said. "I will admit to thinking the case was over when you nabbed Julio Almas—another part of the case you should have never been involved in, Wise. But you were intuitive enough to see through that. Yes, you damn near killed a man before you were absolutely certain if he was the killer, but in the end it seems you might have saved a life. One of those recordings of his made it clear that Wendy Hudson was next."

"I have to apologize again," Kate said. "I had the hunch but wanted to be sure before I informed you. But as you know, I never really got the chance."

Duran waved it away. "You caught a killer, Wise. I don't keep up with this sort of thing, but that makes more than fifty for your career, right?"

She shrugged. She had honestly never kept up with it, even when other agents had whispered about her numbers and accolades in awed reverence.

"This case proves one thing to me, Wise. The fact that you still managed to get results—even after everyone else around you was saying the case was closed—shows that, fifty-five or not, your mind is still as sharp as ever."

"Thanks…I think."

"I've spoken with the other directors," Duran said. "We want you back. We can get around the rules, find a way to get you a waiver to come back for one year. See how you feel then. We know you're bored with retirement. And we need you. And clearly, you are as capable now as you were one year ago when you left. What do you say?"

Kate nodded. She wanted to jump at the offer right away. But in the back of her mind she thought of Melissa, of Michelle…and even of Allen Goldman.

I'm going to call him when I get back home, she thought, the idea random and foreign in Duran's office. *I'm going to call him and take him up on dinner. And if he tries to kiss me, I'm going to let him.*

She wondered why the thought occurred to her. And then she realized: it was a yearning for life. For real, normal life. For the chasing killers to end.

And yet, as much as she yearned for it, she also yearned to be back in the action.

She felt torn.

A part of her was tired. But another part, the stronger part, needed the action.

"Can I think about it?" she asked.

"Yes. And if you take this, I'd like for you to partner up with DeMarco indefinitely. She needs you, too."

"Thank you, sir."

DeMarco looked over to Kate with a sleek kind of smile—a look that said: *The ball is in your court…*

For a moment, Kate found herself thinking of Jimmy Parker and Logan Nash—the first partner she'd worked with and the last before her retirement. Jimmy had been her mentor and Logan had looked to her for guidance in some areas. Looking to DeMarco, Kate wondered if it might be time for her to close the circle—to be the mentor and teacher to DeMarco in the same way Jimmy had helped her through her first few years.

Not that DeMarco wasn't already a stellar agent. But being chained to Violent Crimes for so long and then being let loose in the field, she would be an exciting partner to work with.

She thought of Melissa one more time, her daughter who was seriously seeking a career in the FBI, a career Kate had modeled for Melissa's entire life. The thought made her maternal instinct kick in. But honestly, it also excited her quite a bit.

She took her leave and left through the small waiting area in front of Duran's office. Before she made it to the hallway, DeMarco caught up to her.

"You'll come back, right?" she asked.

Kate smiled.

"I just might be too stupid to let it go," she said.

DeMarco laughed. It was a sweet sound, coming from the throat of the woman who had saved her life two days ago. DeMarco had gotten away with just stitches to her forearm and Kate had managed to get away with nothing more than a severe bruise along her back. And here they were now, laughing about it.

If it was a sign of things to come, Kate thought her year of retirement might just become nothing more than a foolish decision that shrank further and further away in the rearview mirror of her life.

The future, all of a sudden, bloomed brightly ahead on the horizon.

Book #2 in The Kate Wise mystery series is coming soon!

Blake Pierce

Blake Pierce is author of the bestselling RILEY PAGE mystery series, which includes fourteen books (and counting). Blake Pierce is also the author of the MACKENZIE WHITE mystery series, comprising ten books; of the AVERY BLACK mystery series, comprising six books; of the KERI LOCKE mystery series, comprising five books; of the MAKING OF RILEY PAIGE mystery series, comprising two books (and counting); and of the KATE WISE mystery series.

An avid reader and lifelong fan of the mystery and thriller genres, Blake loves to hear from you, so please feel free to visit www.blakepierceauthor.com to learn more and stay in touch.

BOOKS BY BLAKE PIERCE

KATE WISE MYSTERY SERIES
IF SHE KNEW (Book #1)

THE MAKING OF RILEY PAIGE SERIES
WATCHING (Book #1)
WAITING (Book #2)

RILEY PAIGE MYSTERY SERIES
ONCE GONE (Book #1)
ONCE TAKEN (Book #2)
ONCE CRAVED (Book #3)
ONCE LURED (Book #4)
ONCE HUNTED (Book #5)
ONCE PINED (Book #6)
ONCE FORSAKEN (Book #7)
ONCE COLD (Book #8)
ONCE STALKED (Book #9)
ONCE LOST (Book #10)
ONCE BURIED (Book #11)
ONCE BOUND (Book #12)
ONCE TRAPPED (Book #13)
ONCE DORMANT (Book #14)

MACKENZIE WHITE MYSTERY SERIES
BEFORE HE KILLS (Book #1)
BEFORE HE SEES (Book #2)
BEFORE HE COVETS (Book #3)
BEFORE HE TAKES (Book #4)
BEFORE HE NEEDS (Book #5)
BEFORE HE FEELS (Book #6)
BEFORE HE SINS (Book #7)
BEFORE HE HUNTS (Book #8)
BEFORE HE PREYS (Book #9)

AVERY BLACK MYSTERY SERIES
CAUSE TO KILL (Book #1)
CAUSE TO RUN (Book #2)
CAUSE TO HIDE (Book #3)
CAUSE TO FEAR (Book #4)
CAUSE TO SAVE (Book #5)

CAUSE TO DREAD (Book #6)

KERI LOCKE MYSTERY SERIES
A TRACE OF DEATH (Book #1)
A TRACE OF MUDER (Book #2)
A TRACE OF VICE (Book #3)
A TRACE OF CRIME (Book #4)
A TRACE OF HOPE (Book #5)

CPSIA information can be obtained
at www.ICGtesting.com
Printed in the USA
BVHW041515120521
607123BV00010B/160

9 781640 297937